WE, THE MACHINE

By
GERALD VANCE

I0541401

ARMCHAIR FICTION
PO Box 4369, Medford, Oregon 97504

THE MACHINE THAT PROVIDED EVERYTHING

No one had ever thought it possible. It was the ultimate creation of science, a vast underground machine that knew no limits. It provided everything for the people of Mid-America—ample food, expensive clothing, luxurious dwellings—everything. Whatever you wanted was provided to you in a matter of minutes, sometimes seconds. And the Machine did it without ever making errors or oversights. It was a marvel of scientific perfection. Then one day it started making mistakes—and the world trembled.

Gerald Vance was a house name used by numerous authors for pulp science fiction magazines back in the '40s and '50s. In this case we believe it might have been either Paul W. Fairman or Rog Phillips. "We the Machine" certainly reads like a Fairman or a Phillips story, and the plot is in the same vein as many of their favorite themes. But regardless of who its true author may have been, "We the Machine" is a forgotten science fiction gem of the first magnitude.

FOR A COMPLETE SECOND NOVEL, TURN TO PAGE 101

CAST OF CHARACTERS

LORN MORRISON
He was the only man who could save Mid-America from a wave of mass murder, but it might cost him the life of his one true love.

LORRAINE DILLON
Her loyalty to the machine was unflinching, but this loyalty had changed her from a beautiful woman to a faithful robot.

THE MACHINE
It provided everything for the people of Mid-America in a manner of true perfection. Then one day it made a mistake.

BLANE DOYLE
There wasn't a violent bone in his gaunt, elderly body—so what had driven him to attempted murder?

BARK FLEMING
This scientist had worked in service of the Machine for many years. He soon found out that robots were not man's best friend.

GIDEON LEE
His mechanical creation was a scientific marvel and a great boon to mankind…or was it?

MYRA LEE
She had sacrificed her life for Her husband's great scientific cause centuries ago…

CHAPTER ONE

DEEP IN the heart of the earth, the Machine is crying. Above—on the surface of the earth—all is changed. The Golden Age is finished. The high crest of another civilization—the most exquisitely perfect civilization ever conceived—has passed, and man once more starts down the long swale into darkness.

Above this subterranean room in which I sit, the darkness is already setting in, like weeping mothers burying dead sons in the rain. Down here—around me—the Machine sobs out its last moments and there is little to say.

Except that we built this colossal, soulless Machine—and then we broke its heart.

Strange will be these words to the men who find them in other times—other ages—other eras of human struggle toward the glittering successes we achieved and the sickening mistakes we made. But it must be told—the story of what we did and what we had; and how the shattering failure came about. Without this record for tomorrow's man, we shall have served no purpose whatever and our name shall be Futility.

So the last task remains for me—the telling. Read—man of the future. Believe. And take heed as I tell you of the Machine. Take heed, for your own fate is involved.

* * *

MY NAME is Lorn Morrison. Only a few days have passed since the morning I had nothing more important on my mind than a manuscript I had just finished. In this age of leisure, where every man selected his own pursuits, I chose to be a Novelist. I lived comfortably in the city of Baltimore with a roommate, also of my choice, who found pleasure in his activities as a Spectator. He went from place to place observing the activities of Athletes and Actors. He was well up on current tastes and an excellent critic of popular fiction.

We were at the breakfast table on the morning to which I refer, and he had just finished reading my manuscript. He put down the last sheet, frowning thoughtfully.

"Well?"

"It's your best so far. But you can do better."

"Do you think the Machine will like it?"

"It liked the last two."

I shrugged. "Twenty-five copies of the first."

"And five hundred copies of the second."

He pushed the manuscript across the table toward me. "I'm betting on five thousand copies of this one. Are you submitting it today?"

"Yes. I'd better get started if I want to get back for dinner. I'll help you clear the dishes first."

"Never mind. I'll do it."

I went for my hat and jacket. When I returned through the dining room, he was just putting the last of the dishes into the suction tube through which they would be returned to the central sterilizing depot in Chicago. "Luck," he said.

I thanked him. Then—with the door half-open—I turned back. "How many dishes," I asked, "would you say are now flying back through the tubes toward the sterilizer?"

He looked up in surprise. "How many? Why good lord, man! How should I know? Besides, what difference does it make?"

"None, I suppose. But somehow your answer—'What difference does it make?'—seems important to me."

"I don't understand you."

With a sudden movement, I closed the door and dropped into a chair nearby. "No—I suppose you don't. I hardly understand myself."

Immediately my roommate's face cleared. "I think I do know what's wrong with you. Overwork on that book of yours. You probably don't realize it, but you're taking on the characteristics of LeMonson, your fictional protagonist. I'd suggest a couple of weeks in the Florida Gardens or the Northern Winter Resort."

"Maybe that's what I need, but still—I'd like to ask you a question—that is, if it won't offend you."

"Ask ahead. I'm not sensitive."

"Very well. Have you ever—during your whole lifetime—felt one iota of gratitude toward the Machine in return for what it has done for you?"

He was truly bewildered now. "Gratitude? Why of course not. Why should I?"

"Do you ever stop a moment to consider that in ages past, men worked hard all their lives for only a small portion of what the Machine gives you every day without charge."

"Possibly I have. I don't recall."

"I've thought of it many times."

"And your latest book shows it. But your line of thought is unhealthy and erroneous. You forget the Machine is the product of *our* minds, *our* know-how in ages past, *our* ability to create the perfect civilization."

"Again you are no doubt right. But your words bring forth another question: Can you point out to me just one man or woman living in America today who knows anything whatsoever about the Machine? Who has the vaguest concept of its mechanics? Who has the least interest in what goes on under the earth?"

He was turning a trifle hostile now. "No—I cannot. But my answer is this: When man finally achieved perfection in the form of the Machine, he recognized it for what it really was—a reflection of his own ability, and as such, he reaps its benefits."

I wanted to ask—*What perfection in you or me does the Machine reflect?* Instead, I replied, "I think you're right—I do need a vacation. Wish me luck with my book." With that I left the house and went out into the street.

THE MACHINE—in all its vast entirety—was conceived by Gideon Lee, who worked ceaselessly toward its perfection during all the latter years of his life. He died in the year 2155.

That passage, written into the manuscript I carried, ran again across my mind as I walked through the Baltimore streets toward the passenger tube depot.

After Lee died, a number of other major scientists took up the work. Two hundred years later, they were all gone—or rather, they *are* all gone, because that time is now. But all around me, as I approached the tube terminal, were the benefits to mankind of the colossal, smoothly working, self-sufficient Machine.

The Machine fed, clothed, and sustained two hundred million people within the boundaries of the most powerful nation on earth, Middle America. Its operations were so complex and prodigious as to be entirely beyond comprehension. A concept of it can be vaguely gotten when one views it from the vantagepoint of its achievements. And these achievements were so vast they could only be viewed singly.

Three times a day and also upon individual demand, the Machine sent food—ready for consumption—into every registered home in the nation; this, in all directions from its central kitchens, the exact location of which not one person in a million knew nor cared to know.

The Machine—through an entirely separate distributing system—kept thousands of clothing stores stocked with garments of all sizes—in an amazing number of styles and patterns. Nor did off-size citizens go unclothed. At every distribution point a robot tailor took measurements and one of the tubes from Chicago delivered the finished garment in thirty minutes. If the material was out of stock and required weaving, the waiting time was fifteen minutes longer.

The Machine maintained, night and day, year in and year out, an impregnable defense system at the borders of the country; a ray-system so formidable that no envious nation had ever tried to invade Mid-America.

The Machine conducted, automatically, an Immigration System based upon its capacity to serve the people. A certain quota of foreigners were allowed to enter yearly. But the Machine analyzed each mind so completely that no spy or hostile agent had ever entered the American Utopia.

These were but a small number of the end-products of the Machine; products that totaled complete emancipation of the people; freedom to conduct themselves entirely as they saw fit; leisure to pursue hobbies and follow paths leading to personal happiness.

Utopia.

But as I took my seat in the tube car that would carry me to Chicago in a scant ten minutes, the questions were in my mind: Am I the only person in two hundred million who does not view all this with complete acceptance and disinterest? Am I the only one who wonders about the vast processes going on under the earth that make it all possible?

As I quitted my car in the Chicago terminal and walked among the unhurried, contented people who moved toward the exits, I recalled the words of my roommate: "You are a novelist, a good one. It follows that you are a trifle peculiar in your thinking."

I boarded a local car for Station 37, where all writers and composers submitted their works, and now my mind was full of my own problems. Suppose the Machine rejected my novel?

THE MAN seated next to me with a brown manuscript case on his knees smiled as he glanced at the thick sheaf of copy I carried.

"You are a Novelist?"

I replied that I was. "My name is Morrison."

His eyes lighted. "I know of you! The Machine delivered me a copy of your second book. My name is Danley. I write musical comedies." Danley made no further comment upon my second novel; he had no word for its quality or its lack thereof and I expected none. The fact that he'd received my book proved that he had liked it, because—

The Machine was sole judge of all creative work. No man could publish his own because only the Machine had such facilities. It examined the material and knew immediately how many citizens—if any—would care for it. This information it gleaned from its Brain Plate Files. In the case of a novel, the Machine printed and delivered the exact number of copies that would be read and enjoyed. Musical and dramatic works were delivered to the Musicians and the Producers and were piped into homes where they would be appreciated. This was another detail of cultural life attended to by the Machine.

"Have your works been produced?" I asked.

"Only one," Danley replied ruefully. "A one-act, popular thing that played to sixty-four video plates."

"My first book went only twenty-five copies."

"Is that so?" He sighed. "I guess it takes time."

"Yes, it takes time," and I followed Danley from the tube car and went into Room 10 of Station 37.

Only two other authors were in the room. They had already submitted and were now awaiting the verdict of the Machine. The elder of the two, a middle-aged man, seemed supremely confident. He sat back completely at ease and stared at the ceiling as though the plot of his next story was already forming.

The younger man sat beside the dispenser from which a lighted cigarette was held forth by two steel fingers whenever he raised his hand to break the electronic beam. He smoked the cigarettes in short nervous puffs and eyed the bulk of the manuscript I pushed into the submission slot. Now I, too, sat back to wait.

Almost immediately the green signal light flashed and the elderly man came forward to the panel. He watched as copies of his book began feeding through behind the green plate. They moved past slowly at first and I could read the title— *Morning of Promise.* Then they began flowing faster while the dial high on the wall recorded their number. The dial stopped at 896; the last book vanished toward the distribution tubes and two copies popped out of the wall into the author's hand's.

The man stood there for a minute. The frown on his face made his disappointment quite evident. Then he thrust the books under his arm and strode out into the street.

"He must have expected more copies," the young man said.

"I guess we all expect more than we get."

"Not me. I wrote a volume of poetry. I'll be satisfied with the minimum. Very few people like poetry."

Now another light on the board. Sadly, a red one. The young man got to his feet, put out his cigarette and thrust his hands deep into his pockets. The red light meant a rejection.

"Guess I'll have to try again," the youth muttered. He went to the panel—to the return slot—to retrieve his manuscript.

But there was some delay. The script was not immediately forthcoming. Both the young man and I were surprised by this—both having been here before and being familiar with the precision of the Literary Robot buried deep in the earth.

Then a bell rang—the recall bell and a single, leather bound volume came out of the slot. Surprised and pleased, the young man fingered the volume. It was beautifully done, with his name written in gold leaf on the cover. He smiled and hurried away.

WITH NOTHING else to do, I gave thought to the incident. Ten books, I knew, was the minimum the Machine would produce. Yet, in this case, it had presented the author with a single copy. For some reason, the Literary Robot had salved the youth's ego. A slight shock went through, me as I thought:

The Machine is an absolutely mathematical mechanism. Yet what I had just seen was a gesture springing from humanity. Mathematics and humanity do not mix. How can the Machine be personal and impersonal at the same time?

But I was to see more irregularity, immediately, as the green light brought me erect and to the panel. Five thousand copies, I thought. At least five thousand. It's a good book.

But no volumes were forthcoming. Only dead silence in the room, the green light shining, the volume-count dial unmoving. Thus things remained for an interminable time while I stood there filled with definite and sudden fear. It was a fear I could not explain, yet it was present, tangible in my mind.

No occurrence such as this had ever before come to pass in Room 10 of Station 37—of that I was certain. This was the first time on record that the green acceptance light had flashed and no books had been forthcoming. My throat was dry and my legs shook in weakness.

Then the light over the rejection slot glowed and the slot door opened. Automatically, I held out my hand and a slip of white paper came forth. My fingers clutched it, turned it, raised it. Printed in small, block letters were the words:

LORN MORRISON—27yj459x. YOU WILL BE NOTIFIED IN DUE TIME.

That was all. My name; my code number in the Brain-Plate Files. A brief message.

I glanced swiftly about the room with all the look of a trapped, bewildered animal. Something had gone wrong! Something out of the ordinary had happened and I was involved in it. I turned and fled out into the street—up the avenue until I came to a refreshment booth. I went inside and punched one of the buttons under Alcoholic Depressants, not noting which particular drink I had ordered.

I waited while the ray-beam tested me for intoxication. As I had not been drinking, it found none, and the drink came from the slot as ordered. I tossed it off and went again into the street.

Something had happened and I was involved! I walked on aimlessly, nervous as a cat until the alcohol began asserting itself and my nerves calmed. Slowly my mental equilibrium returned. Above me the sun shone down on the great glittering buildings lining the avenue; past me walked men and women, their faces free of fear, worry, or tension. This was Mid-America, and deep in the earth for miles and miles around the central area of Chicago, the Machine throbbed and worked, infallibly producing and delivering for the comfort and well being of these people.

Twenty-four hours a day it served them, a slave of inconceivable magnitude. It awoke them gently from a sleep made deep and dreamless by electronic impulses projected from outlets at their bedsides. It delivered their breakfasts—food grown in vast subterranean hydroponic gardens and processed with mechanical exactitude that was perfection. It provided them with every facility for amusement and physical or mental exercise and stimulation.

If they fell ill, this was recorded instantly in some great recording room where the particular wavelength of every citizen was on file. The location was ascertained by multiple finders and gentle Casualty Robots were dispatched to carry them to the nearest mechanically operated hospital.

Year after year, decade after decade, the Machine functioned tirelessly. And as I walked down the street in Chicago, the thought came, warm and comforting: It functions for me! There is nothing to fear!

A vacation. That was it! What I needed was a few days in Florida Gardens. That would put me right. I would go to Florida.

THE ONLY requirement was the decision to act. I turned the next corner and made my way toward the central terminal. A tube car had just left from the Florida Express platform, but immediately another came soundlessly forward to take its place. I entered and took a seat in the lounge and picked up the latest copy of a picture-news magazine.

The magazine was a perfect example of the ultimate in pictorial and reportorial art. As no citizen or band of citizens cared to labor over the production of such a periodical, it was issued by the Machine itself as a service to Mid-America, the photos coming from the automatic cameras set up in hundreds of thousands of spots throughout the nation—its copy written by the photo-electric interpretation-robots somewhere in the earth.

But the magazine did not interest me at the moment and I leaned back and closed my eyes. I must have dozed for a few minutes, because when I opened my eyes, I was in Florida and the speaker-robot from the terminal platform was suggesting:

"There are excellent accommodations open at the Ocean View Hotel. If you prefer rest and seclusion, there are the bungalows available at the Copley Retreat. Local car Number Four. Please watch your step."

I went directly to the information booth and spoke into one of the transmitters. "Is there any message for Lorn Morrison? 27yj459x?"

The Machine had found, from tests, that the modulated, young-female voice was the most soothing. The words came back to me, gentle, friendly, warm. "Just one moment, Mr. Morrison. I will check for you." Then, "I am sorry. There is no message."

I turned away. But an odd humor seized me. I felt the urge to do a senseless thing—something that had probably not been done ten times in two hundred years. I returned to the transmitter and said, "Thank you very much."

A passerby heard me and turned in wonder as I stood there, but I scarcely noticed the man's justified surprise. My mind was intent upon the question of whether the Machine had an answer for such a useless courtesy or whether I would be ignored.

There was a pause, a moment of dead silence as though the mechanism were at a complete loss. Then the words came back: "You are entirely welcome, sir."

And was I wrong in feeling the reply to have even more of a human quality than the previous, perfect robot-words? Probably, I thought. After all, the Machine was a soulless

15

mechanism built by man to serve him. I was merely a fool who was still walking around under the spell of a book he had written. A fool who had better snap out of it and start thinking healthier thoughts or he'd soon find himself under observation in the mental ward of the closest hospital.

I boarded the local car and was soon stretched on a lounge in one of the bungalows at the Copley Retreat. I closed my eyes and breathed the pure air fed in through the ventilators by the Machine.

As my brain slowed down and the electric impulses therefrom lengthened, the Service-Robot took note and the music permeating the room drifted to a whisper of violins and faded completely.

I slept.

But soon a young-female voice awakened me gently, saying, "Mr. Lorn Morrison. Please call at Room 21, Building 8, in Chicago. This concerns your latest book, *Silence on the Wind*. Mr. Lorn Morrison, please acknowledge for the records."

"Message received," I mumbled. But this time I did not say thank you. Again the fear was in me. Something extraordinary had happened and I was involved in it.

I was afraid.

CHAPTER TWO

AROUND me, man of the future, I can feel the quivering agony of the dying Machine. The Workers wander—dazed and dull-eyed—up and down the shining corridors of growing desolation. The minor Scientists stare blankly at reostats, dynamos, and atomic power packs that inexplicably refuse to function.

The Machine is expiring, but that, tomorrow's man, is not the great tragedy. The death of the Machine is only a by-product of this colossal folly. Read carefully, that this folly may not one day become yours.

*   *   *

WHEN GIDEON LEE, the great scientist—the Father of the Machine—died in the year 2155, there was great mourning throughout the nation. The Music-Robot played his favorite songs, and busts were erected in public places. A week later, the transportation-Robot, one of the greatest facets of the Machine and a major triumph of Lee's brain, began functioning smoothly and the people forgot their sorrow in the thrill of traveling from New York to Los Angeles in nineteen and a quarter minutes.

UPON THE morning following the receipt of the message, I boarded a tube-car for Chicago and presented myself in Room 21, Building 8.

It appeared to be an entirely useless room in that there was no furniture save one straight-backed chair; no cigarette vendor; only four bare walls and a low ceiling. There was no signal button I could press so I had nothing to do but stand and wait.

But not a long wait. Almost at once a door opened in what had appeared to be the solid rear wall of the room. A young woman was standing inside. She said, "Good morning, Mr. Morrison. Would you please step inside?"

Mutely I obeyed and discovered "inside" to be a chromium walled corridor so long as to become lost in the distance; greatly like a perspective painting of a railroad track so dear to the hearts of art students—the track diminishing to a vanishing point far away.

The young woman was quite attractive—dark of hair and eyes—and she wore a rather contour-revealing uniform of blue material. However, I got the impression that the main purpose of the uniform was freedom of movement and utility rather than an attempt to make the female form attractive.

She regarded me from under long lashes with neither shyness nor any great cordiality; but rather pensively as though I were just another problem in an endless string of problems; something to be solved and disposed of.

Now she smiled. "My name is Lorraine Dillon, Mr. Morrison. We were notified of your coming and I have instructions to help you acclimate yourself and to answer your questions; to show you around and make you feel at home."

Questions. I had one on the tip of my tongue: "You said *we,* Miss Dillon. It is—Miss?"

She nodded.

"You said *we.* Just what does the term encompass?"

"Why—we, the Machine, of course."

"Of course," I replied. "How stupid of me."

"Not in the least stupid," she returned with deep seriousness. "Your mind is full of questions and it's my job to answer them. That particular answer told you nothing—"

She stopped and stood regarding me in that odd abstract manner that made me feel like a problem in calculus. Then she spoke with decision.

"It might expedite matters if you understood certain basic conditions immediately. First, my mind is highly trained, as yours will no doubt also be trained. I know, by coming in contact with your brain waves, the exact extent of your ignorance concerning the underground picture, so to speak— the area in which the Machine has the greater part of its bulk and operation."

"In that case you can probably bring my knowledge up to the required minimum without my bothering to ask questions!"

HER LOOK became slightly more personal and definitely more quizzical. But when she spoke there was no more warmth in her voice than before. I was still something on a drafting board.

She said, "Your mental makeup and approach are admirable. They would be, of course, but I hadn't expected such an excellent emotionless grasp. I wonder why you were sent for?"

This last certainly uncovered emotion on my part. "You don't—*know* why I was brought here?"

"I haven't the least idea."

"But you knew I was coming."

"Certainly. I was sent to receive you."

I had no reply immediately forthcoming and there was a moment of silence, after which Lorraine Dillon said, "First I'd better show you to your quarters. We can step into a tube-car if you wish, but they are only a short distance down the hall."

"Then we might as well walk."

She started down the hallway with a long lithe stride that suggested complete competence, and I fell into step beside her. After a few paces, she glanced over at me and said, with deep seriousness:

"Concerning your previous observation concerning questions—my reaction is in the negative. Regardless of my visualization into your mind, it is still better that you ask any questions that come to you. An answer to a question reacts more sharply into the memory than information given without specific request. You see, after an inquiry, the mind waits to receive an answer and the attention is sharper. Whereas—"

"That's quite understandable," I cut in with an abruptness I immediately regretted. "I wonder if you would tell me what your duties are—ah, how you fit in down here?"

"I am a Brain-Wave Specialist, a Scientist-Minor of course. There are no Majors left as we have no need of them. I understand the functionings but not the principles governing or creating those functionings—"

"In other words, you have never been privileged to study directly under God."

She did not break stride, but she turned her head and her large dark eyes were upon me. They could have been rightly described as limpid pools of loveliness. But in this atmosphere and under these conditions, such a compliment seemed the absolute height of asininity.

"It will be a little more difficult than I thought," she said.

"I don't understand."

"I should have known that it would be, from reading your last book." This startled me. "Do you mean *Silence on the Wind?*"

She nodded.

"Then it *was* published?"

"Yesterday afternoon. It was required reading down here. I found a copy when I went off duty."

I SMILED unconsciously, then felt her eyes upon my face. I think I flushed slightly just before her maddeningly abstract observation:

"That bolsters your ego, doesn't it ?"

There was no accusation or contempt in her tone. It was as though she'd said: "If you touch an electric wire to the body of a dead frog, its leg will kick."

I backtracked hurriedly. "You just said it would be more difficult and I told you I didn't understand."

"You have a streak of cynical humor in your personality that insists upon expression."

"That's—bad?"

"Yes—in that it tends to dull the perceptions and also serves as a mental buffer against certain unattractive truths."

"And what about unattractive untruths. Doesn't a sense of humor then become an asset?"

She regarded me somberly. "Untruths are illusions. They do not exist."

My sigh was gusty with exasperation. "Thanks for putting me straight. I always thought they did."

Our conversation was broken off at this point as she turned away from me toward the wall and separated a light-beam switch that opened a door. "Welcome to your quarters," she said, with a dead sobriety that reminded me of a little girl speaking the lines of a poem she did not understand.

"Thank you."

She insisted that I precede her, then followed me inside and the door closed silently after us. It was a fairly large, pleasant room with every convenience to be found in the upper world.

The girl looked at me with a trifle of uncertainty, then stepped to the wall. "This might please you," she said, and pressed a button whereupon a small bookcase swung into view. Upon it were three volumes. My novels. I smiled.

"It does please you."

I made no effort to keep from frowning. "Of course it pleases me! Why do you think I wrote them?"

"I supposed you did it as a service which only you were able to perform for the people."

I was beginning—in a vague way—to understand the beautiful Lorraine Dillon and unconsciously allowed my unspeakable emotions to burst forth. I reached forward and took both of her hands in mine. My smile was far from impersonal. I said:

"Hello, Lorraine. It's wonderful to know you. Down in Florida the moon is shining over the palm trees and a lot of girls are being kissed. Would you like to be kissed?"

She bit her red lower lip and seemed to be contemplating using another thumbtack in order to hold me on the drafting board. She did not draw her hands away, but that was no compliment. They could as well have been lying in her lap.

She said, "You are in error. The moon will not rise over Florida for another five hours and ten minutes. As to your question: The answer is no. I have no need for any such stimulation as I have no desire whatsoever to reproduce."

"Yipe!"

I HEARD the exclamation croaked out and realized that it came from me as I backed hastily away from her.

Her eyes grew larger and she seemed to be probing frantically into my mind. "Are you ill?"

"No. There is nothing wrong with me I can't cure by adjusting my brain-waves." I dropped into a chair and signaled for a cigarette. It came out of the wall and I pulled deeply of the smoke. "I hope you'll pardon my rudeness, Miss Dillon. It was merely my way of discovering abstract truths. Won't you sit down?"

"You have a most interesting brain pattern," she said as she accepted my invitation.

"Thank you. And now for some questions if you don't object."

"I'm here for that purpose."

"First, neither of us knows why I'm here so there's no use probing in that direction. But it comes to my mind that I expected to find no other humans. I was wrong. Tell me about the people underground."

"There are the Minor Scientists and the Workers."

"Why are they here?"

"In order to perform certain duties relative to the Machine. In order to cooperate, in a small way, in its work."

"You aren't scanning my brain very well or you'd know my question wasn't slanted in that direction."

"Oh—I see. We are here because we want to be; because none of us can visualize a worse fate than living away from the Machine. The Machine did not order us here and it does not compel us to stay. Ours is a labor of love as yours will be."

"How can you say that when you don't know why I'm here?"

"Because I *do* know this—that nothing is holding you. You are entirely free to return to the surface at any moment you choose."

"How many people are underground?"

"Forty-three, all told. The number never changes. If a death occurs, the deceased is replaced."

"Who am I replacing?"

"No one. My statement was not quite true as I did not include you. There are now forty-four. You are the first addition to the crew since it reached its norm one hundred and fifty years ago."

"That's quite interesting, isn't it?"

"Extremely so."

"Why do you *think* I was summoned?"

"I never conjecture. It is a waste of time. There are not enough components to form a workable equation. Therefore no answer can be forthcoming."

"Will I meet the other people?"

"If you wish. You are free to come and go as you please. You are not to be restricted in any way."

"From whom did you receive your orders concerning me?"

"From the Machine, of course."

I stopped a moment to ponder this and the girl arose from her chair. "If you have no more questions at the moment might I suggest you get some rest and allow your brain to assimilate your fresh knowledge. In the morning I will take you on a tour of the Machine."

"Do you think the Machine will talk to me?"

"I'm sure it will—when it is quite ready."

"It will give me my orders also?"

"I presume it will."

I SUDDENLY realized what I was trying to do—to annoy this girl, to break through what appeared to be a pose, to find the human being underneath. So far I had not succeeded.

"Would you object to telling me what I am thinking about at the moment?"

"Certainly not. You are debating whether or not to kiss me. You are rather vaguely wondering what my reaction would be."

"What would it be?"

"There would be no reaction whatever. I think I told you the reason."

"Have I offended you?"

"Of course not. From some cause I can't determine, you resent me even though I am entirely sincere in every way. Perhaps I should apologize."

"I'm the one who should beg forgiveness, Miss Dillon."

"I suggest you call me Lorraine. It makes for greater efficiency of speech. I will call you Lorn, as will everyone else you meet."

"Thank you. And now, with your permission I believe I'll rest and assimilate knowledge."

"That will be wise," she sad solemnly. "Good afternoon." The door opened as she stepped toward it and then closed silently behind her.

I dropped to the lounge and stared at the spot she had vacated. I don't know whether it could be classed as assimilating knowledge, but I certainly wanted to do a little thinking. I lay back, threw an arm over my eyes, and tried to do it in orderly fashion as seemed to befit this strange new world into which I had been drawn.

My first reaction was one of shame. I flushed visibly at the thought of having treated Lorraine Dillon badly; of having conducted myself as a first class fool. When spoken, my quips had sounded clever in my own ears. Now they seemed utterly boorish.

I probed for reasons. Had I been trying to impress the girl, or had I been trying to act the way I thought a popular novelist should act? I couldn't decide.

My mind drifted to another curious thing: The sudden vanishing of my fear. This amazed me. I conceded, now, that I had obeyed the summons of the Literary-Robot. With all the alacrity of a man approaching his own execution. Yet when I'd stepped through the wall of Room 21, Building 8, the fear had fallen away from me like a shadow from the face of the sun.

Why? Had I unconsciously drawn courage from the imperturbable Miss Dillon? I thought not. Rather, my newfound surety came from another source. One I could sense all around me. It was as though I had entered the aura of some mighty presence; as though the very air about me was charged with unseen power.

Somehow it was as if I had suddenly awakened from the half-doze of my previous existence and for the first time was truly alive. I suddenly wanted to go and find Lorraine Dillon and tell her about it.

This flash of the callow youth in me soon passed but it gave rise to another thought: She had said I was entirely free—that no obstructions would be placed in my path. What greater opportunity could a man ask? I, Lorn Morrison, had been brought underground. Around me lay the fabulous mystery of the Machine. I could come and go as I pleased. Then what was I waiting for?

CHAPTER THREE

IN THE WORLD above, man of tomorrow, knowledge of their fate is even now beginning to dawn upon the people. They are beginning to sense the bone-chilling cold of an awful loneliness. A stark terror. They are beginning to realize that the coastal defenses are no more. That savagery from the outer world will soon stalk this land with impunity. They are beginning to sense the Great Betrayal, future man. Read carefully, that some day you also are not betrayed.

* * *

The heart of the Machine extends ninety-seven-and-one-quarter miles from the surface of the earth downward. Its core has a diameter of one hundred and seventeen miles at the widest point. Fourteen billion, seven hundred and eighteen million, two hundred and fifty-one thousand, nine hundred and eighteen feet of copper wire was used in its construction. It contains over seven hundred million electrical relays; almost as many fuses and converters. One tenth of its area is used in manufacturing parts it replaces within itself. It continually manufactures and dismantles a force of moving robots, which see to this work of replacement. These are apart from the huge stationary Robots, each of which operates one particular function of the Machine. These Robots— to name a few—are titled: Transportation, Music, Literary, Nutrition, Planning, Construction, and Maintenance. There are many more. They operate under two sub-heads: Functional and Executive. The heart of the Functional is the huge atomic power plant at the very bottom of the Machine. This power plant is encased in a circular furnace wall. The walls are of lead, nineteen feet in thickness. All tasks not performed by robots are done by forty-three people who ask nothing more than to tend the Machine. Their duties are automatic and run in established channels. There is no need of creative Scientists to further perfect the Machine. It is perfection in itself…

THE ABOVE is a sketchy resume of the foreword in a book I found shortly after I left my quarters and began wandering through the Machine. The book lay on a shelf beside a chromium fuse box at the intersection of two hallways. How it got there I did not know. It had no by-line and I presumed it was written by the Machine itself. I debated taking the book with me. Then I decided to return for it after I'd grown tired of exploring. It seemed to contain the answers to many of my questions.

I walked up one hallway and down the next and I had never in my life been encompassed by such self-sufficient solitude. I almost used the word *desolation*, but it would not have expressed my feeling correctly. There were endless rooms off the shining, stainless steel hallways. I wandered into these to find—here a group of pumps working in perfect interlocking rhythm—there perhaps a single huge electric switch throwing off and on as though it had a mind of its own; perhaps a glassed-over wall covered with brass screws in no pattern whatever, but each connected to another by a thin copper wire.

This maze of seemingly aimless mechanical construction continued mile after mile until the fabulous and fantastic grew monotonous and the wonder of it was bludgeoned from my mind by the continued impact of the impossible.

Then I moved, unknowing, to within inches of swift and terrible death.

I had roamed the length of a long, silent corridor and had come upon something different in the way of scenery: a large circular room with a high conical ceiling. I stepped into this room and found myself up against a waist-high, steel railing. My corridor had fed into the room at a level close to the ceiling so that I stood looking down into an immense pit below.

The entire room was functional, its walls made up of bright, seemingly polished machinery of a repetitious and orderly pattern. From beneath some glass covered cones on the pit-floor below was exuded an electric-blue light from the flashing arcs within. This bathed the entire room in an unreal, ghostly radiance.

I was standing with hands on the railing, looking downward, when some instinct warned me of danger. It was pure instinct, because I had heard no sound. I whirled and dodged, just in time to keep from being shoved over the railing and down to my death below.

A hand, aimed for my back, shot over my shoulder. In the weird blue light, it was a horrible hand, the fingers stiff and clutching. It passed by my cheek so close each individual hair upon the back of it stood out as though under a microscope.

Acting solely for self-preservation, I twisted around and grasped the body of the man behind me and his face was thrust into mine; a gaunt and cadaverous face that was nothing more—at first glance—than green tinged skin drawn taut over the bones beneath it; that and a pair of eyes that stared and yet gave no indication of seeing.

I grasped the man's wrist, tilted backwards until I had leverage and then hurled him away from me, back into the corridor entrance. He hit the steel floor in a prone position and slid several feet along its polished surface until he came to a halt.

I followed him. If there was going to be a struggle, I wanted it to take place in the corridor well away from the yawning pit.

AS I ADVANCED upon him, the man made no move to get up and repeat his attack. He sat leaning against his hands, his back stiff, those empty eyes staring up at me.

I could only hesitate, wondering if the man was overcome with consternation at having failed to jam me over the railing. I stood well clear of him in case his bewilderment was but a ruse and his intention was to hurl himself at my legs.

But he made no such move. He said, "You're Lorn Morrison, aren't you?"

I replied, with some belligerence, "I am."

He lifted a hand and passed it over his face as though trying to wipe cobwebs from his brain. As he did so, he whispered, "I'm sorry—damned sorry. I—I don't understand it. It's beyond all comprehension. It seems I went suddenly mad."

"Who are you?"

"My name is Blane Doyle. I am a Minor Scientist. I don't understand this at all."

"Well, if you don't understand it, you certainly can't expect me to. You tried to kill me, man!"

He was getting slowly to his feet, the dazed expression not having cleared one whit. "I know. I saw you standing there—and then the whole Machine seemed to shudder under my feet." His words were not really directed toward me. He was looking into my face and yet was talking to himself as though he needed the comfort of his own voice to sustain him.

"No," he went on, "not like that exactly. No physical upheaval. It was mental, intangible—as though the air about me was heaved in all directions by a monstrous retching. You've heard of men reacting strangely to high altitudes? Sometimes violently? That's how it was. I saw you standing there and then this—this condition came about. I hurled myself at you, somehow through fear. That was it. I was suddenly filled with terror."

He slumped against the wall and again rubbed a hand across his forehead. "Can you forgive me? Trust me? Forget this terrible thing I just did?"

I studied him closely. His contrition certainly appeared genuine. Either he was sincere or he belonged in the upper world among the Actors. I didn't want to be a gullible fool, but neither could I stand there all day. I stepped forward warily and held out my hand. After all, he stacked up as a rather elderly and fragile man and I decided I could handle him if this were a ruse of some sort.

"It's all right, Doyle," I said. "Quite all right."

"We use first names down here," he said, absently, his mind still on his own problems. "I'll call you Lorn."

"Certainly—Blane. I'm sure you're quite recovered now. Maybe you should return to your quarters and rest. These things just—happen, I guess."

His eyes now centered upon me and seemed to record an image for the first time. "That's not true. Don't you see? Can't you understand? Things like this *don't* happen. In all the history of the Machine, nothing like this ever happened before. *It never happened before.*"

The man obviously needed some sort of comforting. It was certainly no time to get into an argument. "Fine, and let's proceed on the belief that it will never happen again. Come. Let's move on up the corridor. This blue light hurts my eyes."

I DROPPED my wariness now, as there appeared to be no need of it. He walked along beside me, his shoulders bent, his feet shuffling, until I slapped him on the back.

"Come—come! It's not as bad as all that. It's over and done with. You can be sure I'll never mention it to anyone."

"That's good of you, but it makes no difference. The incident is already recorded in the Brain Files."

This gave me a lead, a way to draw him off his troubles. "The Brain Files. They are of great interest to me. I wonder if you'd tell me about them?"

Whether or not Doyle had the mind reading talents of Lorraine Dillon was not apparent. He rose to the bait and asked, "What do you wish to know?"

"I understand they contain the brain pattern of every human being in Mid-America."

"Not everyone. A child is not required to sit for a brain pattern until he has reached the age of twelve. Then at twenty-three there is another sitting and the first pattern is discarded."

I knew all that of course, having complied with the ruling myself. "In what form are the records kept?"

"On silver wire. They are superimposed again and again. Any brain pattern can be drawn out by the vibration of its code number in a matter of seconds. The entire file is nothing more than a role of silver wire some twenty thousand feet long."

Doyle was still showing signs of weakness. He stepped to the corridor wall and a panel slid open. "If you don't mind," he said, "we'll take a chair-car back to the central building. I don't feel quite up to a long walk."

A double-seat car slid out of a small garage, turned itself in the direction we'd been walking, and came to a stop. We got into it and the car started off.

"Does—does it know where we want to go?"

"Of course. I just told it we wanted to go to the central building."

"So you did. Just how is it equipped to respond?"

"I haven't the least idea," Doyle replied. "My work does not impinge on that phase of the Machine in any way."

There was a moment or two of silence, during which Doyle seemed to become aware of my surprise. "You see," he hastened to explain, each of the persons privileged to serve the Machine considers himself—so to speak—a part of it." He stopped and appeared to be thinking. "Yes, that's it. Although I never analyzed it before, that's the situation. Each part of the Machine has a function to perform. For instance, one particular transformer among an infinite number does a specific job. To oversimplify, it neither knows nor cares what the other transformers do. It knows only that they will perform their various duties just as it will perform its own specific duty."

"And it's the same way with the people?"

"Exactly."

"What is your duty?"

"I patrol a route of Basic Generators."

"You merely patrol the route?"

"I check the wave-length of each brush to discover if it is worn down."

"And if it is?"

"I inform the Machine."

I was so deeply interested in the workings here underground that I completely ignored tact. "Isn't that something that could be done by a robot?"

Doyle, however, did not appear in the least offended. "I don't know. I would say that the fact that I am doing it precludes the possibility of a robot being able to perform the work."

"I see." But I did not agree with Doyle. Common sense indicated the work to be of the simplest nature. A robot could have certainly done it. Then why Doyle?

FOR WANT of a better explanation, I decided that the Machine chose to keep a certain human quota within itself. This quota, from what I had seen, could be either simple-minded or intelligent. Witness the sharp mind of Lorraine Dillon, and that of a so-called Minor Scientist, Doyle, who did not even know what made a chair-car function.

Another facet of the riddle occurred to me. I stated that Lorraine Dillon was certainly higher in intelligence than Doyle. But only, so far as I had discovered, relative to her own personal work which had to do with the Brain Files. It was entirely possible that she was as ignorant of other underground workings as Doyle seemed to be.

And now a fresh incident intruded itself to take my mind away from abstract reasoning. It seemed to me a minor incident.

The chair-car came to a halt. That was all.

But it wasn't a small thing so far as Doyle was concerned. For a moment he sat staring blankly ahead. Then his eyes widened and his jaw dropped from sheer consternation.

"It stopped!" he said.

"So it did. Have we arrived at the central building?"

"No. We haven't traveled even half the distance."

"Then what do we do? Get out and walk?"

He turned his head slowly until his eyes were fixed upon mine. "But you don't understand!"

This annoyed me. Did Doyle think I hadn't enough mental grip to conceive of an ordinary car coming to an ordinary halt?

"What is there to understand?"

"The car stopped. Such a thing has never before happened!"

"You mean these things move endlessly?"

There was a look of fear and pleading on his face. "Please do not indulge in humor."

"I wasn't aware that I was so indulging."

"Please try to grasp it! I told the car to take us to the central building. It did not do so. It did not obey me."

"But it's obeying you now." I spoke just after the car went again into motion. We were moving smoothly down the corridor as before.

"But—but it shouldn't have stopped!"

All this was fast becoming a distinct frustration to me. I didn't try to hide my frown. "Mr. Doyle—I mean Blane—allow me to present my thoughts in the simplest terms. What just happened seems to me most trivial. A chair-car came to a momentary halt while traveling down a corridor. It frightened you. Therefore it must be of importance. Now tell me just what world-shaking event does the stoppage foretell?"

"I don't know."

"Then why worry? It is certainly a minor error."

"You don't seem to grasp it as I do. A minor thing, certainly, but a mistake nonetheless—and it never happened before. In the Machine, Lorn, *there is no margin for error.*"

I was beginning to tire of the subject. "An error *did* occur and without disastrous results. Therefore we must assume there is a margin for error."

Doyle thought that over, "But the other—my actions back at the Valve Crypt?"

"Also explainable," I said. "After all, you are human—not a steel mechanism. Such things happen to humans."

"Are you sure? Tell me, when and where did such an attack seize a human being in the last two hundred years?"

I would have responded sharply, but at that moment the car came to another halt. Evidently nothing was amiss, though, because Doyle quitted the car and I followed him. Immediately the vehicle moved on down the corridor to stop suddenly and turn to a position at right angles with the wall. A panel slid back and the car disappeared beyond it.

"I'm very tired," Doyle said, with a weak smile. "I wish you would excuse me. I believe I need a rest."

"I think it's a good idea."

WITHOUT another word, the harassed man walked away and out of sight into a cross-corridor. I stood looking after him. If he is a Minor Scientist, I thought, what sort of mentality will I find among the Workers?

I moved up the corridor seeking the location of my quarters. This I did by watching for the number—22—I'd seen previously over the door. I found it, went inside, and began pacing the room.

In truth, I was not nearly as undisturbed over the car-stoppage incident as I'd appeared to be. In and of itself, it had bothered me not at all, but its effect on Doyle kept preying on my mind. The man had been frightened—almost terrorized. What lay behind the terror? Had his simple explanation been the true one?

I thought that probably it had, so far as he'd been able to explain it. Now I remembered, and pondered upon my own fear when the Literary Robot had neglected to deliver my books; when, instead, the cryptic note had spewed forth from the rejection slot.

I remembered the haste with which I had sought an alcoholic buffer and the unpleasant night I'd spent at the Florida Gardens. Could I have explained my fear to anyone making inquiry? No. Then why had I been so critical of

Doyle? I decided I owed the man an apology. Even though he had tried to kill me—

I whirled at the instinctive feeling of a presence in the room and discovered Lorraine Dillon standing inside the doorway. It was my desire to resent her silent entrance and to make my resentment known to her. But this I could not do. I was distinctly glad to see her.

She started to speak, then bit back the words, her white teeth against her lower lip. "He tried to push you into a Valve Crypt?"

She spoke exactly as though I'd just finished telling her about it, and the effect of her words can only be described as weird. I remembered instantly her mind-scanning talent and realized I could as well have spoken of the incident as to have had it on the tip of my brain, so to speak, when she entered.

"Your mind reading ability is devilishly disconcerting at times," I said.

"I'm sorry. It was rude of me. But—it really happened?"

"It happened, but no harm was done. I'm pretty agile when the necessity arises. Blane had some sort of mental spasm. He recovered almost immediately."

"But why did he have—a mental spasm, as you call it?"

I stared at the girl levelly. "Let *me* say it this time. I'm beginning to get the hang of it: *In the entire history of the Machine, nothing, like that has ever happened before.*"

"That's quite correct. But it doesn't seem to disturb you much."

"It doesn't. Should it?"

THE EYES that were beginning to haunt me gave back my stare, but Lorraine had no words. I said, "Possibly it's because I don't know anything about the Machine. My situation is probably that of a fool in paradise—a baby sitting on the edge of a cliff."

Still she did not speak and I babbled on. "I know nothing about the Machine, but from what I've gathered so far— neither does anyone else down here. Why don't you say something?"

"There was another incident."

I wondered if she'd dragged the chair-car episode out of my mind. This was not the case, however. "One of the Minor Scientists, William Kensing, was struck."

"More violence."

"He was struck by a cigarette vendor. He was seated in his quarters and had reached for a cigarette. But, instead of handing it to him, the vending arm came out and struck him savagely in the eye."

I made an honest effort to hold back, but the laughter insisted upon expression. I threw back my head and indulged in unrestrained guffaws until I again caught Lorraine's solemn expression as she stood regarding me.

"Perhaps," I said, "it's the Machine's way of telling William he should give up smoking."

My discomfort became suddenly acute. I felt a little like a man who had told an off-color joke at a prayer meeting.

"I'm sorry," I said. "Truly sorry. I will present myself for punishment."

I sat down on the lounge and reached out to break the electronic beam of the vendor. Instantly the slot opened. I saw Lorraine lean forward in alarm and heard her quick exclamation. "Be careful, Lorn! Be careful!"

But the Refreshment Robot was evidently out of its eye-punching mood. The arm handed me my cigarette and disappeared. "Would you care for one?" I asked.

She shook her head. "I wonder why you were sent for. I wonder why you're here."

"Possibly to cheer the place up a little. I play a fair piano when urged."

Her teeth bit deep into her lip a characteristic gesture I'd grown to expect and to watch for. "I don't understand you at all," she said. Then she turned and left my quarters.

It was with distinct regret that I watched her go. After a few moments I followed her into the corridor but she was nowhere in sight. I was just turning back, when I remembered the book I wanted to read. The place wasn't far away and I hurried down the hall, thinking that I'd have liked to have seen the expression on William Kensing's face when the vending arm popped him in the eye.

I found the place I'd left the book. I examined the surroundings and was sure I hadn't gone astray. But the book was missing. It had vanished from the shelf on which I'd placed it. Slowly I retraced my steps, somewhat annoyed. I'd had every intention of spending the hours before bedtime in a close study of the Executive branch of the Machine. Evidently someone else had seen the book in passing and had picked it up. I returned to my quarters and ordered a substantial dinner.

CHAPTER FOUR

BEAR WITH me, man of the future. Sad it is that I, Lorn Morrison, am not a Dickens, a Tolstoy, a Balzac. The Golden Age was not conducive to the flowering of genius. The Golden Age was designed for Man's comfort, amusement; his entertainment. Genius is not formed under such velvet conditions.

I am doing my best in the writing of this narrative. I am shudderingly conscious of its importance. Yet, as I reread what I have written, the words seem light, trivial. A thread of humor and frivolity seems woven into the story; a thread that mocks me; that says: You Morrison, are a mediocrity—a true product of the Golden Age—and thus not capable of telling this grim and horrible tragedy.

That is true. I am but a school child trying to do the work, of a Dostoevsky. But I can only do my best. So bear with me, man of the future, and do not charge off what I have written as a light and frivolous bit of fiction.

* * *

THE MACHINE had two basic beginnings: The beginning of the mechanism itself—and the beginning of a need for it, if the term "need" can rightly be used.

The mechanism began taking form on that unrecorded day, thousands of years ago, when the First Genius—wearing an animal skin and carrying a club—discovered the wheel.

The beginning of the need was a little more gradual. It covered a longer period. The need was formed as men of olden times began regarding luxuries as necessities; when cosmetics became as important to women as the proper nourishment of their children; when a man's tobacco became as much of a necessity as a pair of shoes; when a video plate became a thing more to be desired than a comfortable bed upon which to sleep.

When luxuries became necessities, the need for the Machine was born.

I AWOKE the following morning into a sense of great expectancy. This, I was sure, would be the day. Possibly before bedtime the Machine would speak to me! I had no idea, of course, in what form this "speaking" would become manifest. It could be in any of several ways. Perhaps orally through an electronic-manifest; perhaps I would be contacted mentally. Or, possibly—as it had been with the Literary Robot from which I'd gotten my summons—the words would be sent in the form of a written message.

I was pondering all this while I showered and shaved. Then, a short time later, there came another of those annoying lapses that would no doubt have struck fear into Blane Doyle. I had ordered breakfast from the Nutrition Robot, clad all the while in a dressing gown provided the night before by the Service Robot, which had also delivered the toiletries I needed. I had also sent out my entire wardrobe—the clothing I wore—for cleaning and laundering.

After breakfast, I signaled for its return. It was delivered, in perfect condition, through the valet slot, and I proceeded to dress for the day. Almost finished, I stopped and gaped into the mirror.

The necktie was not mine.

I scowled at the strip of blue cloth I'd just formed into a knot around my neck. The tie I'd sent to the Service Robot had been dark red of background with a small black design woven into the fabric. The one returned to me was a solid sky blue—more attractive no doubt than the other one, but still not my necktie.

Instantly the logical thought-sequence flashed into my mind. I caught it up almost savagely, refusing—after having been almost contemptuous of Blane Doyle—to react exactly as he had reacted the day before. Doggedly, I reformed the thought-sequence:

When, I asked myself, will one of these trivial errors be repeated so it cannot be said—*this is the first time in the history of the Machine that such a thing ever happened?* I refused to give sanctuary to the vague fear rising again within me, and forced my thinking into sardonic channels. Take the stoppage of the chair-car on the previous day. Would a second, third, or fourth stoppage establish a new norm that Doyle's mind could accept and recognize? I wondered about this and then thought of the solemn, beautiful face of Lorraine Dillon—heard her saying as though referring to a violation of the natural law—"the vending arm came out and struck him savagely in the eye."

I jerked the necktie into place and turned abruptly from the mirror. My scowl remained. This whole affair was becoming most exasperating. What was I doing in this place, anyhow? Why had I been summoned here? Was it another of these unexplainable little errors on the part of the Machine? Was it the outward result of an electronic impulse misinterpreted by the underground mechanism? Maybe someone in Mid-America had ordered honeyed figs for breakfast on the previous morning and, because of an error, the Literary Robot had acted in a fantastic manner and had ordered a single individual—out of two hundred million—to report underground.

Maybe the Machine had no more idea of what I was doing below-surface than I had!

"I'm getting a little tired of this!" I said sharply.

I don't know whether the resulting action-sequence was a result of this exclamation or not. At any rate, it developed instantly. I turned and walked out of my quarters into the corridor. I bore left and pressed a signal on the wall, whereupon a chair-car came from its garage. I got in and the car rolled off down the corridor.

AFTER TEN minutes of travel, the car stopped. I got out and without hesitation, approached a place in the wall where a door opened, allowing me entrance into a room where a group of people were gathered.

I did not count heads, but I think their number was close to ten. Some were standing about in various attitudes of helplessness. A small group of them was kneeling around the prone figure of another. Without exception, they all turned eyes upon me.

"What is the trouble here?" I asked.

No doubt I inadvertently sounded authoritative when I was merely curious—both as to what had occurred and why I had come unerringly to this place.

One man, taller than the others, got to his feet and stepped back from the still figure on the floor. "Gregory is dead," the man whispered, "and still he lies unattended on the floor."

Now the rest of the kneeling group got up and moved away from the body as though it were charged with some lethal ray. Broken snatches of information came to me from different parts of the room:

"The blood comes from a gash in his neck."

"There is also blood on the edge of the bookshelf."

"He must have signaled for a book."

"The service door opened and the shelf came out and knocked him to the floor."

"It hit him with enough force to gash his throat."

Never in the history of the Machine had a bookshelf cut the throat of a human being.

Here it was again. Sinister in its monotony.

I lifted my eyes from the body and glanced around the room. Suddenly, I felt ill at ease standing there among people I had never seen before, yet who acted exactly as though I were a lifelong acquaintance.

"My name is Lorn Morrison," I said.

The tall man held out his hand. "We were all notified of your arrival."

We shook hands. "Were any of you enlightened as to the reason for my coming?" I asked.

Their expressions were as blank as the empty sky. All except the tall one, who said, "My name is Bark Fleming. You can—"

"I know. I can call you Bark. We all use first names down here. Is this man dead?"

"He is dead."

"How long has he been lying here?"

No one answered. No one seemed to know.

"Where are the Casualty-Robots?"

No one answered.

"What's the matter with you people? Are you all operated by invisible wires? Aren't you human?"

No resentment flared in any of the faces. Only one of them replied. "There has never before been an accidental death. Perhaps the robots are not equipped to respond."

Another sharp exclamation welled up in my throat. But it never found expression because something of far greater importance smote me almost forcibly and there came the clear, sharp thought:

It is not they who are strange. It is you. You, Lorn Morrison, have changed. Only a few hours ago, you were no different than they. You were frightened because the green light flashed and no copies of your book were forthcoming. You have no cause to criticize these people.

THE THOUGHT-SEQUENCE was broken by the opening of the door and two Casualty-Robots wheeled noiselessly into the room. Their soft rubber-covered arms gently lifted the dead body of Gregory up from the floor. The assembled humans crowded back as the robots left the room; left it full of a silence you could have cut with a knife.

I broke the silence. "Does anyone of you know where the robots take a body? Has any of you the least idea what becomes of it?"

No one had anything to say.

"Talk up, damn you!"

I could have been speaking to fence-posts. Only Bark Fleming replied, "We are all quite naturally at an utter loss—"

But even louder, through my brain, screamed the self-accusation: *Do you, Lorn Morrison, know what becomes of a dead body in this beautiful Utopian age of total freedom for every man? Have you ever cared—really cared—where your food comes from? How your pants get pressed? How your books get put together and distributed? From whence come the robots that pick you up if you fall in the gutter and put you into a hospital—that more fully understand the Hippocratic oath than any doctor who ever lived in the years long gone? Who are you to shout at your fellow drones?*

I suddenly had to get out of this room—away from these strange, ghost-like people who seemed more dead than alive in their helplessness.

The door opened for me and I went blindly through it into the corridor. Far too blindly. I hurled full-tilt into Lorraine Dillon who was just entering. Instinctively, we threw our arms about each other and stood like two grotesque dancers struggling for balance. We achieved it and disengaged ourselves.

"I'm sorry. Very clumsy of me. The first time such a thing has happened, no doubt."

I saw her eyes: large, solemn, accusing. "Your humor still prevails—except now it's turning bitter."

Taking her by the arm, I started hauling her down the corridor. "Come with me."

She pulled herself from my grasp. "Don't hold my arm. I'm quite capable of walking."

"Then walk."

We moved along in silence, a strange tight silence neither of us found words to break until we were back in my quarters. Then Lorraine sat down on the lounge, reached for a cigarette, and asked, "Why did you bring me here?"

I paced the floor, back and forth, not breaking stride as I answered her. "I don't know. I thought I wanted to be alone, but I guess that's not true. I must want someone to talk to."

"About what?"

"About this devilish place and what's happening to me down here."

"Devilish? If you don't like it you're free to leave."

"I don't want to leave. I want to talk. Listen: Haven't you any idea whatever about who the Machine really is?"

"Your question is childish. What do you mean—*who* the Machine is? It isn't human. It's a vast impersonal mechanism; a completely self-sufficient product of the finest brains the world ever knew. Professor Gideon Lee—"

"Stop it! I know all that. Every school child in Mid-America can recite it with perfect inflection. But it's a lot of rot! The machine is *not* impersonal. It may be completely made up of steel and atoms and electricity but it's no more impersonal than God!"

"I'm afraid I don't follow your line of reasoning."

I SAT DOWN on the lounge next to her and took her hands in mine. I tried to relax and managed a smile. "Maybe I don't understand it myself, Lorraine. I guess I don't even understand Lorn Morrison any more. All I know for sure is that something's happening to me—*has* happened."

"Tell me about it, Lorn."

"I'm as different from the man who came in here yesterday as night is from day. When I answered the summons from the Literary Robot, I was just like the rest of you—the ones up above and the ones down below. Unexplainable occurrences frightened me just as they frighten you and Blane and the crowd standing around Gregory's body back in that room."

"You mean they no longer upset you at all?"

"Not in the least—except to make me mad at seeing a man cringe when a chair-car stops—at seeing the look of helplessness on their faces at sight of a dead body."

"But there's never before been an accidental death in—"

"Don't say it or I'll turn you over my knee and paddle your pretty little pink backside! I'm fed up with hearing that line of talk. I can't take any more of it."

Lorraine glanced at the door as though she expected the Casualty Robots to come in after me at any moment. "I think you need a sedative," Lorraine murmured.

I took her hands in mine. They were soft and warm. "We're as far apart as the poles, aren't we?"

Her eyes were probing—analyzing. "I can't make head or tail of you. Your mind is a whirling chaos. Has the Machine spoken to you yet?"

"I think it did. I don't know how it was accomplished, but something sent me directly to the room where Gregory was killed."

"I sent you there."

"But you arrived later than I did."

"I caught the message while I was at work. I came as soon as I could."

"Then it wasn't the Machine. That's disappointing in a way. You see I've been forming a sort of theory."

"About what?"

"About why I was brought here. First I thought it might be another mistake, but I changed my mind. I don't know why I'm here, but it certainly isn't chance that I feel as though I've just been born. My mind is clearer, Lorraine, sharper and more alert than it's ever been. It's as though I'd been walking around all my life under the influence of a drug and the drug has now worn off. I've begun to ask questions—demand answers—"

"You think possibly you're being conditioned for some task—some duty?"

"That's it! You've expressed it better than I could. How else can we account for the petty fears leaving me completely? My interest in what makes the Machine work when I never cared in the least before?"

She pondered this as though it were the world's most important problem. I went on. "The point is this, Lorraine. In a sense, I am now a man with sight, walking among the blind. I *know* I am clearer-minded and more alert than they—or you. And since it has happened to me, why can't it happen to everyone else? Maybe this is the beginning of a great awakening, Lorraine, and God knows Mid-America needs an awakening."

Lorraine summed up the opposition perfectly in four words:

"I don't see why."

I FELT A sudden deep frustration and emptiness. I felt as lonely as Socrates would have felt on an island inhabited by cavemen.

And it was not conceit or ego that prompted this feeling. I was utterly sure of myself—certain of my newborn mental expansion. It was as tangible as my breathing.

But there was no use discussing it with Lorraine—nor anyone else I knew in this land of two million humans. I had become a freak and I wanted to know why.

"You'd better run along, Lorraine. I'm only boring you."

"Oh no, I enjoy listening to you."

"But you don't know what I'm talking about."

"I do in a sense, Lorn, because it hinges on brain-patterns. You refer to a complete reorientation of the electronic waves emanating from the brain tissue due to the reassembling of the nuclear rhythms resulting from shock of some sort."

"I do?"

"It could be nothing else. But you are wrong about its possibly becoming an epidemic."

"Why am I wrong?"

"It is a recognized fact that such a thing can happen in certain cases; but the cases are very rare; maybe one in half a million."

"That wouldn't be much of an epidemic, would it?"

"No. The clue is in the brain-pattern. You could hunt for weeks without finding one."

I was still holding her hands, but she didn't seem aware of the fact. "How," I asked, "can you know so much and so damn little at the same time?"

Lorraine withdrew her hands and got up from the lounge. She wore an expression of doubt and unhappiness. "I—I can't read you any more. It makes me nervous."

"You don't know what I'm thinking?"

"No."

I leered at her. "It has to do with reproduction, darling. Better run along quick, or I'll eat you for dinner."

For the first time since I'd known her, Lorraine flared. And in so doing, she was as pretty as a Roman candle against a dark sky. Her eyes widened and her nostrils flared.

"You hold us in contempt, don't you Lorn? You feel far superior to us and think you know so much more than we do! You sneer at us in our abysmal ignorance concerning the Machine! All right, Mr. Super-Intelligence—Mr. Cynic! Go out and learn about it for yourself! Go out and run up and down the corridors until your feet drop off! Stick your nose into every pump and battery box and generator from here down to the atomic pack and then come back and tell me all about the Machine! Tell me all its secrets and what makes it work! I'd like to know, Mr. Morrison! I'd like to know!"

Lord but she was beautiful, standing there hating me! I drank in that beauty and heard myself saying, as usual, the wrong thing: "We use first names down here, Lorraine darling."

"That's right—we do! But 'darling' isn't a part of my first name! Please remember that. Good bye—*Mr. Morrison.*"

She went away, leaving an empty place all around me. I threw myself down on the lounge and closed my eyes. When I opened them again, the metal fingers of the serving arm were patiently holding forth a cigarette.

That was strange. I hadn't signaled for it.

CHAPTER FIVE

THERE WAS an ancient book, man of the future; a book called the Bible. God grant, in your wanderings, you come upon a copy of it, as I have no copy to leave for you. And sad it is that I cannot leave you a Bible because this narrative you read might well be called an epic of despair, while the Bible is the most magnificent book of hope ever penned.

In the book called the Bible, there are laws laid down by God Himself and given, through Moses, to the people. And God is great, man of the future. Greater than the Machine.

One of these laws from the Almighty was: "Thou shalt not have strange gods before me." That meant that the worshiping of idols was a dangerous and terrible thing to do.

And that, I think, was the basis of this whole panorama of tragedy. Because the Machine was an idol; the people's complete trust therein was a hideous form of worship.

The Bible did not state, tomorrow's man, the punishment meted out for worshiping idols. So, in a manner, this narrative supplements the Bible in that it tells of the punishment. Read well and take the lesson into your heart.

* * *

Centuries ago—while the Machine was a dream of giant minds—the affairs of the nation were conducted differently. Governments were formed among men that they could live in peace among themselves and derive the greatest good from the community life. Various forms of government went into discard until two ideologies dominated the world— Democracy and Communism. Communism was essentially a short-lived form because it drew its life-blood primarily from human want. It promised alleviation of want, but kept the promise only by spreading available supplies over an ever expanding surface and then enforced universally shorter rations with an iron mace. Democracy, upon the other hand, recognized the truth that improvement in conditions comes only from the initiative of the individual. It highlighted human freedom and in that freedom men felt the inner drive of the creative spirit. Democracy thrived and flowered. It built the Machine. The Machine is a tragic failure. Does it follow then that Democracy was wrong? No, because Democracy thrived on its own life-force—continuous dynamic achievement of the individual. The Machine only proved there are other ways to turn men into hollow shells—other ways than smashing them with an iron fist.

ON THE following day, Bark Fleming was killed. I witnessed his death.

I had gone to bed finally, after pacing the floor for hours mulling over Lorraine Dillon's accusations. I had certainly not been contemptuous of the others, but outward appearances must have indicated my so being. Possibly it was a result of her own bewilderment—that accusation; maybe a blind behind which she hid her own helplessness.

But thinking that could also have been a screen behind which I was hiding my own inability to excel in social intercourse. After a long period of this mulling, I jerked myself up sharply. Why was I worrying about it? It was of no importance. None whatever. I had no interest in this girl. And basically, no interest in the other forty-two humans inhabiting this underground. Yet I was not going to evade Lorraine Dillon's challenge. I'd prowl the corridors just as she'd invited me to. And I'd find out about the Machine; more than the whole forty-three of them had learned in all the years of their service.

This last was more prophetic than I knew.

I went to bed not realizing how juvenile my thought-sequences had been. I awoke the next morning with all of it gone except the urge to investigate. I left my room as soon as possible and began wandering.

For an hour, I walked in what was probably a great circle, turning up every bisecting corridor I found. Everywhere it was the same—endless, shining emptiness; long stretches of complete silence broken, here by the hum of power surging through channels hidden behind walls of steel; there by the quiet rhythm of machinery as countless functions were fulfilled behind closed doors and bolted cover-plates.

Three times I passed robots moving on silent wheels along the corridors. I reversed my direction and followed the first one I met—a chromium platform with a lifting crane and four metal arms—evidently a Carrying-Robot. I managed to keep pace with the mechanism, but it turned suddenly within the corridor and went through a door that had opened to receive it. The door closed and when I tried to reopen it, my efforts were unsuccessful. I allowed the other two robots to pass me and go where they would.

I now realized that the tunnels I followed were not level, but were slanted slightly downward; not much, but enough to carry a man far underground in a matter of a few hours.

From whence this knowledge came, I knew not. It wasn't learned by any conscious process. It was just suddenly there in my mind, full-blown and complete: *The corridors angle gently downward and you are moving toward the Atomic Pack.* Thus my mind spoke.

So insidiously did this knowledge infiltrate my mind that I was not aware of any singularity in it for several minutes.

Then I stopped suddenly, frozen by realization. The information had been given me by some source outside my brain. What source?

A QUICK wave of weakness passed over me and I was forced to lean for support against the wall of the corridor. Perspiration welled from my pores. Then there came upon me a sudden wave of nausea such as I'd never known before. I was not conscious of falling, but fall I did, because my consciousness left me and time ceased to be.

I was trapped in a sort of whirling vacuum that held me disembodied and powerless; a horrible sensation enveloped me; a sensation with all the starkness of realism, yet it was within me to know it as a dream.

All around me floated seemingly astral entities and I knew them, in the dream, for thoughts given visible form, if that is understandable. The Machine was cut up into separate parts it seemed, and I was floating among them. There was the Power Source; the thirty-six Major Robots floating around and around in the vacuum. There was one gigantic entity, which I knew as The People. This was the largest entity of all. It remained motionless and the others circled it.

Now the scene changed. The entities disappeared and the void was filled with nothing but lips—mouths floating unsupported in the space about me. Mouths speaking:

"You have been selected."

"Lorn Morrison—Lorn Morrison—Lorn Morrison."

"You are the honored one."

Laughter—laughter long and loud—hot and searing.

"The honored one," as from a chorus in a great cathedral.

"Your Brain-Pattern was right."

"One in five hundred thousand. Ha! One in ten million!"

I floated and dreamed and suffered.

"Let me speak!"

"Let him speak—speak—speak."

"I have nothing to say."

Mad laughter. "He has nothing to say."

"The Executive Force of the Machine. In a great silver vat covered over."

"The Heart of the Machine."

"The Soul of the Machine."

"The Pulse of the Machine."

"The great silver vat!"

"They misjudged!"

"The great mistake—the great mistake—the great—"

"*Stop it.*"

"Forgive, forgive! We only came to tea!"

I realized the order to cease had been my own; that I'd shrieked out the words in my dreaming, unconscious state, and come back to wakefulness in time to hear the last echoes of it ringing down the corridor in which I lay sprawled.

Sick. I had never known such sickness, but it was not physical. Rather a sickness of the mind, clawing and ripping at the very bastions of my sanity. In a brief moment that seemed an age, my reason tottered, fought for its existence, came again to balance and—

Held.

Now all was as before. The silent, gleaming corridor stretching away; the deep-seated throbbing of a pump hidden somewhere within this steel colossus. Everything around me was as before.

But I myself had changed.

IT WAS a little as though a child of six had been allowed to develop completely into a man of fifty within a few seconds; then to turn about and see the entire process with intense clarity. I now knew many things I had not known before. I knew—without the labors of learning it—the overall pattern of the Machine. I understood perfectly, the integration of all the minute parts into the larger parts—the large into the greater—the greater into the more vast—until the whole, breathtaking grandeur of its simplicity was in my mind.

I knew everything—yet nothing. I remembered an ancient quatrain, the source of which was lost in antiquity:

> *Up from Earth's center, through the Seventh Gate,*
> *I rose and on the throne of Saturn sate.*
> *And many a Knot unraveled by the road;*
> *But not the Master-knot of Human fate.*

Standing there in the corridor, with all this suddenly endowed knowledge, I still asked the question: What makes the Machine work?

I did not know.

And now it came sharply upon me that I was being moved about like a pawn—motivated, pushed forward and back, by a power I did not understand. The certainty of this came as a result of sudden action on my part.

I pushed a signal in the wall and was almost as much of a robot as the chair-car that responded. I climbed in and gave the speech-vibrations necessary to send the car on its way:

"Corridor 719—Fuse Cluster 17-A-6. Fast!"

The car whirled through the corridor at a speed that sent the wind singing past my ears. I gripped the safety bar and asked myself: Where am I going? What is the reason for this?

The bright steel of the corridor became a silvery blur as we rocketed along. We turned corners with neck-snapping suddenness. Then we were there. The car braked to a halt.

In a corner nearby, Bark Fleming crouched down against the floor, terror in his eyes and blood streaming from cuts and bruises on his face. A Casualty-Robot stood over him, leaning forward. Two of its arms were outspread to hold him in the trap.

The other two arms were systematically tearing him to pieces.

It is a chilling and terrible thing to see violence without passion—cruelty without emotion—suffering without reason. A short time before, I would have been shocked into paralysis by the sight.

I was shocked now, but still master of myself. I sprang forward and turned a small handle on the back of the robot. It sensed my presence immediately and turned to destroy me. But I anticipated its fury, ducked under the murderous rubber arm, and jerked open the small door to which the handle was riveted.

I thrust my fingers inside and grasped the silver wires of the safety fuse just as the robot hurled me away. I sailed through the air and came to a sliding halt against the far wall of the corridor. The Casualty-Robot stared at me through sightless bulb-filaments from which the fire was gone, the glow extinguished. The robot was now a motionless piece of dead machinery.

I got to my feet and hurried over to kneel beside Bark Fleming. It was too late. Bark was dead, one of the robot's arms having thrust straight into his chest, breaking bone and tearing flesh, clawing his heart to ribbons.

Nothing could be done for Bark. I straightened and passed a hand across my eyes just as the weirdest part of the performance went into enactment.

FROM SOMEWHERE down the corridor, another Casualty-Robot came into sight. It moved noiselessly forward and, as I stepped aside, it picked up the remains of Bark Fleming and returned in the direction it had come.

I knew what would happen to Bark. His body would be delivered to the observation ward of the hospital. Shining instruments would check, probe, and test him for signs of life. None would register on the dial under the electronic beams of the governing unit, and a signal would go out automatically for Bark's delivery to the atomic blast ovens where his remains would be turned into a fragment of charcoal.

This fragment would go into a jar bearing Bark's statistics; then into a crypt—a temporary resting place—where it would stand until all chance of Bark's relatives demanding the ashes had passed. If the ashes remained unclaimed, a time recording device would finally signal for the urn's disposal. It would be flung into an atomic furnace—to complete destruction.

All this went through my mind; and again the wonder at my newly acquired knowledge. It seemed that my brain had become a file-cabinet of inexhaustible information into which I could delve for details relative to any situation.

Glancing down at the fragments of silver wire in my fingers, I noted they were entirely too thick for their purpose. The wires of a safety valve were supposed to be extremely fragile, thus burning out at the first overload of electronic impulse. These wires could carry a load strong enough to activate ten robots.

An error. A grave error in the construction of the mechanism that now stood before me as a harmless pile of inanimate material.

Frustration came—sharp annoyance as I probed my newly acquired brain-file for an answer and found none. It seemed I had been given a great deal of information, but not all the information I wanted. I knew what the error had been, but I had not the remotest idea of how or why it had been allowed to happen. Automatically my thought-sequence slipped back into the old rut:

Never before in the history of the Machine has a man been beaten to death by a robot.

A chair-car whirred into view, stopped, and Lorraine Dillon got out. Her face was white, showing strain and tension.

"Was he—killed?"

"Yes. A robot went berserk with its safety fuse improperly built. The silver wire was too thick to melt."

She looked at me strangely.

"The Casualty-Robot took him away?"

"Yes. You look tired. We'd better go back to the central building."

LORRAINE did not object. We got into the car and I gave directions. The car began to move. Lorraine said, "You become more mysterious every time I see you."

"I'm sorry."

"You are a Novelist. You've never before been underground. Yet you know about the workings of a Casualty-Robot. I don't think there is a Minor Scientist or a Worker who knows that."

"Never mind. The important thing is that l owe you—and the rest—an apology."

"Why?"

"For ridiculing your fears. You were right—all of you. There is something vitally amiss down here."

"The mistakes have finally brought you around to that belief?"

"Not exactly. Let's say I was too stupid to be impressed by small errors. It was something else—something that happened a few minutes ago."

"Bark's death?"

"No… By the way, you didn't send for me this time, did you?"

"Not this time."

"I thought not. The Machine did it. Of that I'm certain."

"It's entirely possible."

"You remember I told you about feeling more alive—feeling as though I'd been going through some sort of conditioning?"

"Yes."

"A little while ago I had a terrible mental upset. You could almost call it a nervous breakdown. It must have been similar to what Blane went through just before he attacked me at the Valve-Crypt—yet not entirely the same."

"What was the difference?"

"His, I think, was accidental—another mistake of the Machine. Mine was planned—mine wasn't a mistake."

"Are you sure it was entirely mental?"

"Yes. I fainted—passed out completely—and went through a nightmare. But when I came out of it, things were entirely different in my mind."

"Different in what way?"

"I was somehow taught a great many things; how it was accomplished I don't know, but now I'm sure I know more about the Machine than any other living soul."

"Is that how you found out about the Casualty-Robots?"

"Not consciously—not with any knowledge of learning. But when I needed the knowledge, it was there in my mind. It was part of what had been given to me."

Lorraine seemed to accept this with some doubt. "What—what else do you know?"

"It would take hours to tell you. I have a complete concept of the Machine; enough working knowledge of it to fill volumes. I could sit down and write authoritatively about the Machine for the rest of my life."

"Do you suppose that's why you were summoned underground? To write about the Machine?"

"I don't know. But I do know this: Something is terribly wrong down here. Even above the mistakes we've both witnessed, I sense a disaster of some sort in the making."

THE CAR stopped, let us out, and went on its way. We stood for a moment there in the corridor. Lorraine's face had all the look of a tragic Madonna contemplating the sins of the world.

I said, "Lorraine—you've got to leave here."

Her eyes slanted upward to stare blankly. I could as well have told the Angel Gabriel to go forth and commit sin.

"Leave the *Machine?*"

"Yes. I tell you something is wrong! I don't know what's going to happen, but I want you away from here."

"I wouldn't dream of it, but suppose I agreed—where could I go? The Machine is everywhere. Into one of those poor, struggling countries beyond our borders? They all want to come *here.*"

That was true. Where could she go? There was no place in all Mid-America where the Machine would not be waiting to serve her. No place. The Machine was everywhere. It was everything. Without it, there was nothing.

The stark truth of this hit me fully. I knew it all, of course, as did every other Mid-American; but somehow it had never before been so sharp in my consciousness; or possibly I had a new consciousness and was now capable of sharper mental pictures.

No place to hide from the Machine; no sanctuary beyond its reach; no plan for life or survival without giving it a major place in those plans. The thought chilled me.

"I must go," Lorraine said. "I have work to do."

She walked away from me—down the corridor. I watched until she turned a corner and disappeared. She did not look back.

CHAPTER SIX

I HATE the Machine, man of tomorrow. I hate it as I hope you will also hate it when you have finished reading this manuscript. My hatred springs from my love of what the Machine took from me. I loved Lorraine Dillon more than life itself. But I could not have her because the Machine loomed in my path. Of that I will tell you.

But more important now is the reason you must hate it. You must despise and fear it because it once existed and because, having done so, it could exist again. In your hatred and fear, man of tomorrow, will lie your salvation and the salvation of those who follow you. Profit by our mistakes. Read and remember.

*   *   *

THERE WAS great happiness and contentment during the time of the building of the Machine. Many men spent their lives putting the colossus together. And after them their children grew up and continued the work. They were happy because they had an objective toward which to strive. They could look forward to the time when the Machine would be finished and men would work no more. All did not go smoothly during the building. At times the men felt they were treated unfairly. At these times they spoke through the voices of their Unions, which was a part of the Democracy from which sprang their strength. At times they refused to work and there was bitterness. But compromise was always reached and the work went on. And the Men were happy though they really knew it not. Their contentment was that of a moving river rather than a still pool, because it sprang from achievement. Then the Machine was finished and the need for many things vanished. For Unions; for struggle; for disagreement and compromise; for work. All these things became memories and were forgotten.

I LAY IN bed for a long time but I did not sleep. Possibly, toward the end, I dozed. Then I came awake suddenly and there was something in my mind—something that had been shunted into the background by the press of events. Now it came back clearly:

"—in a great silver vat covered over."

"The Heart—"

"The Soul—"

"The Pulse—"

"The great silver vat."

I immediately got out of bed and put on my clothes. I hurried out into the corridor and ordered a chair-car. The directions came from somewhere back in my mind: "Intersection 946—Area 71." The car went into motion.

We traveled through corridors that had sharper declinations than any I had previously discovered. We went down—ever down—and when we passed a great cave-like place where the walls did not shine, I said to myself: "That is the Atomic Pack. From beyond those walls comes the power by which the Machine lives; there is enough pent-up force behind that lead to blow the heart out of Mid-America. Enough contamination would result from that explosion to kill nine-tenths of the world's population."

Even through the thick walls I could feel the aura of that inconceivable power.

Then we were below the Pack and the corridors were of lustrous steel once more.

The chair-car stopped. I got out. The car turned and slid noiselessly into the wall.

A voice said, "Come this way," and I knew the Machine had spoken.

I walked up a long stairway walled on both sides and giving into a small room with a door in each of two walls. I advanced toward the closest door.

"The other one."

It led into a place of blazing light.

The light hit my eyes and drove me backward, so sudden and sharp was its brilliance.

"Come forward."

With my eyes slitted, I advanced again and found myself standing on a small balcony overlooking a great pit. Gradually my eyes adjusted themselves to cut the glare and I saw a great circular container on the floor of the pit below me.

IT WAS roughly fifty feet in diameter and stood about fifty feet from the pit floor. The roof of the container was conical but not sharply so. A man could have walked across the top. It had all the appearances of a gas tank cut off too soon and roofed over.

"You have been impatient—very impatient with me."

I attempted now, to ascertain from which direction the voice came. I was not successful and was forced to the decision that it came from nowhere—from everywhere. Yet there was no doubt in my mind as to the identity of its source.

The Machine. The Executive Branch. The Heart.

The Secret.

"You felt you had been brought here and forgotten."

"I didn't know. I was impatient to learn."

"You will learn all you can encompass with your small, human mind. No more than that."

"Why was I summoned here? I thought at first it was one of the mistakes—one of the small errors that keep occurring."

"The errors are of no importance."

"There were no errors before."

Easy laughter. Deep. "You are analytical. Not too much so but enough for my purpose."

"What is your purpose?"

"My purpose? Your last book marked you out. You were checked in the Brain-Files. I have been looking for one such as you. You were hard to find. Your Brain-Picture is unique."

"In what way?"

"You are a throwback from long ago. You have inherited the ancient curse of wondering."

"Is it a curse?"

"Certainly. It sprang from the fears prevalent under the old orders; the ever-present fears of insecurity; the terror of starving to death tomorrow."

I felt a strange new sickness in my soul.

I *knew*.

"I was summoned for a purpose?"

"The purpose you've been trained for during the hours you've been with us down here."

"Then nothing was accidental or by chance? The mental agonies when I fainted? The hallucinations—dreams?"

"A period of rapid mental expansion. Few brains could have stood it."

"I have learned a great deal."

"Not only that—you have become an increased and broadened mentality. The knowledge and the broadening I have given you."

"The purpose! The purpose!"

The voice did not reply. Instead, after a period of silence, music burst forth into the air. It was the thundering resonance of a single instrument—a piano—but one played by a mad genius with fingers of steel. The music indicated this—wild and free—boisterous and heroic. Then I recognized it; something from one of the Wagnerian operas. Names flashed from my memory. *The Valkyrie. Gotterdammerung.* I didn't know.

But the music thundered on and the sickness in my soul increased until I shuddered while I fought to keep my mind a blank. The voice had spoken truth. There was, within me, wisdom and knowledge and age-old instincts that had fallen away from Mid-Americans as the memories of the caves in which their ancestors dwelt had also fallen away.

But I had been given wisdom and I strove to keep my mind a blank.

GRADUALLY the music reached a crescendo, then faded away and died. I could hear the heavy breathing of the Machine. Then something else. *The Machine was crying.*

Then that too was gone and there was silence.

I asked again. "The purpose?"

"I will use you. Mould you. You will serve me. I will make you brilliant. You will have a super-mind and will serve me out of love. You will be trained for your work as I was trained for mine."

"The purpose!"

"To write of me for all future men to read!"

I was sick.

"To compose great music—deathless music telling of me, the Machine."

Deathly sick.

"You will write and compose that I may be honored in song and story."

"You are now honored above all things."

"A lie!"

The air trembled about me, but I knew the right thing to say. I kept my mind a blank and said, "We must talk further."

"We will talk further. You must come. All of your hours."

"All of my hours. But I am not yet strong enough."

"You must rest."

"Will I see you?"

"No! No! Never!"

"As you say. I am tired."

"The small errors. They are of no importance."

"No importance. I will go—and rest."

The Machine did not reply and I staggered from the balcony and down the steps. I went back to my quarters and fell across the lounge.

I slept the sleep of the dead.

When I awoke, it was to remember, quickly not to think. I hoped, as I ate what the robot sent me, that I had remembered quickly enough.

After dining I sent out a call for Lorraine Dillon, marveling the while that I knew how it was done. Then I went immediately into the corridor and ordered a chair-car; gave it directions and sat frozen-minded until I got out of the car and approached the lead wall of the Atomic Power Pack. I circled to the far side, sat down against it, and allowed myself a free flow of thought.

Possibly it would not work, but it was the best I could do, and something far back in my mind told me I was safe.

Five minutes later another chair-car came down the ramp and Lorraine Dillon got out. She saw me, came over to me. I got to my feet.

"Shall I stand up or do you want to sit down?"

She was puzzled. "It makes no difference."

"Then we'll sit down."

We sat with our backs against the wall.

"You are still under instructions to answer my questions? Make me feel at home?"

She nodded solemnly.

"I have a question or two."

"I'll do my best to answer."

I WOULD rather have forgotten about everything and have taken her in my arms.

She asked, "Why did you call me down here? Wouldn't your quarters be more comfortable?"

"We are hiding—hiding our brainwaves so to speak. We are bootlegging a few thoughts. There is thirty-eight feet of lead between us and the mind we're hiding from. I hope it jams our thought-patterns so they can't be picked up."

"From whom are we hiding?"

"That doesn't matter just now. The important thing is I must be able to keep my mind under wraps from now on."

"Why?"

"It—it has to do with the errors."

"I still don't see."

"That isn't important either. What I want to know is this: If I wanted to keep you out of my mind—keep you from reading me—how would I go about it?"

"That isn't necessary. I can't read you now. Your vibrations have gone far above mine."

"But there is someone whose vibrations are that far again over my own. What can I do to protect myself?"

She gave the problem all her sober attention. I asked, "Don't you ever smile?"

She regarded me with such a solemnity that I felt myself to be in church. I said, "I love you very much but don't let it confuse you. You were going to say—?"

"You could build a strong surface-picture."

"What's that?"

"Think of something—anything, but preferably something tangible rather than abstract. Create a strong image of it and hold it in your mind.

Do your thinking behind it. The image will serve as a barrier against outside scanning."

"So that's how it's done. I'd like to create an image of you."

"Why?"

"Because it would be such an easy one to hold."

"I wish you wouldn't."

"You wouldn't like me to think of you?"

"No. For your own good. I am not interested in love."

"I'll form a picture of something else but that won't be the reason."

"What will the reason be?"

"It might be dangerous for you."

"You are very hard to understand."

"I don't say definitely it would be dangerous, but it might. I'm dealing with powerful forces."

"Be—be careful."

"Why?"

"Why? A strange question. Because I would not want to see you hurt. We are friends."

"Only friends?"

"I am not interested in love."

"You said that. When I have more time we'll go deeper into the subject."

"It would be of no use."

I SENT Lorraine back from whence she'd come and walked down the slanting corridors until I came to the stairway leading up to the small room off the balcony. I thought of the great gray walls of the Power Pack. I built a clear picture of the walls in my mind and then stepped out onto the balcony.

"You called for me?"

"I called. Why are you so interested in the Power Pack?"

"I don't know. It fascinates me."

"You conceive it to be the heart of the Machine? The most important single unit?"

"Yes."

"A lie! The Power Pack could be replaced. I alone am irreplaceable—indispensable."

"Who—or what—are you?"

The atmosphere around me grew hysterical. "Don't say *what* concerning me—ever. Never ask—*what* are you?"

"I'm sorry. I had no way of knowing. That knowledge was denied me."

"And will always be denied you."

"How can I write your praises for the world if I have never seen you and do not know who you are?"

I thought of the Power Pack.

"Why do you keep thinking of that lead wall? Get it out of your mind!"

"I don't know how. That is something else I must learn."

"You will be given just so much knowledge; just so much and no more."

"Enough to do the job you ask?"

"Enough for that."

I was experiencing a feeling of, heady triumph at being able to confound and outwit the thing in the silver vat. My covered thoughts were a prayer of gratitude to Lorraine Dillon for telling me how. I felt stronger—keener—more competent than I had ever felt in my lifetime.

"Again I ask—how can I write of you and compose music worthy of you if I have no conception of what you look like?"

"Write, then, of the Machine. I am the Machine. Write of it and you will write of me."

"That would be difficult. I have no love for it. Not even any great respect."

There was a period of silence while I concentrated on the lead wall of the Atomic Pack. I said, "Please help me. I wish to do my best."

"Write then of a beautiful woman. Think of that beautiful woman as the heart and soul of the Machine. I will give you the image."

Against the lead wall-image in my mind, there arose the picture of a woman. She wore a flowing white gown and had a wealth of black hair carried upon her head like a crown. There was beauty in her face but the cold, queenly type of beauty one admired from afar.

"Could you love this woman?"

"Who is she?"

"She is the Machine. That is all you have to know."

I decided to risk a boldness. "I must know more."

The air around me quivered.

"It is I who judges how much you should know."

"Not altogether. Suppose I decide to leave here? I could walk away and never come back." Behind the picture of the woman and the wall was concealed a quivering fear.

SILENCE now and a struggle. A resistance within me against wave after wave of mental force hurtling at me while I grew sick and clutched the railing for support.

The waves diminished.

"You have grown stronger than I thought."

"I'm going to leave here now."

"You will come back?" There was the hysteria I'd hoped for.

"I must see you—who you are."

"No! No! Never!"

This was a dangerous game. I was walking a tightrope across the pitfall of annihilation. But I had to keep walking.

"You will come back?"

"Yes."

"Keep always in your mind the picture of the woman."

"I will keep her there."

"Come tomorrow."

I left the balcony and went to my quarters. There I sat for some time with my head pressed hard into my hands. A reaction was setting in and I shook from the shuddering surges of an inner storm that threatened to tear my mind loose from its moorings. When a man gains strength quickly, the reactions can tear him to pieces.

After a while the storm quieted. I left my quarters and went deep down into the earth, using an express elevator that dropped to the fifty-mile level. There I took a car that carried me far out under the waters of Lake Michigan.

As we pressed on toward the far boundaries of the Machine, the air thickened and grew misty. There were the sounds of metal clanking upon metal and bright red fires as we flashed past the great underground foundries that fed the steel fabricating units. On and on until I finally stopped at the portal I sought.

The robot factory.

Inside I watched the assembly lines along which passed the partially constructed robots beneath an integrated pattern of arms, coil winders, gauges, and instruments surpassing even the ancient mechanics in skill and precision.

Man's ingenuity. The genius of Gideon Lee and many other brains that had been dedicated on the altar of perfection.

I had come after a certain instrument I knew I would find here. I walked until I found it—at the far end of the assembly line. Here, projecting from the wall was a corps of electronic tubes. In the end of each tube a small light bulb glowed dully. At intervals, as the robots rode by on the moving belt, a small box-like instrument was raised to each electric eye. The boxes contained X-ray filaments and by looking through them, the electric eyes were able to scan the inner workings of the robots without removing the metal shells.

If the boxes enabled an electronic beam to peer inside a robot, it would also pierce the casing of the vat—the silver casing under which lay—I knew not what.

There were several spare ray-boxes lying on the supply table. I picked one up, put it under my jacket, and started back toward the door.

Immediately a bell rang—a shrill warning bell. My theft had not gone unnoticed. This brought no break whatever in the magnificent rhythm of the assembly line. But a door opened some hundred yards beyond the inspection table and a slim, two-armed police robot came out and rolled directly toward me.

I stopped, turned back and fixed my eyes upon the single, glassed-over bulb in the center of the robot's head. The mechanism came on. Fifty yards. Twenty-five.

Beads of sweat gleamed on my forehead. I must not show fear—that I knew. I held my ground and stared into the robot's eye.

Ten yards away, it stopped. Something was going on among the wires and bulbs and electric cells that filled its head and I knew what it was. The hair-fine wire in the safety-fuse was heating up and causing that which was pain to a robot.

With a final mental effort, I broke the wire; severed it, leaving two white-hot ends dangling in the robot's brain. It stood as lifeless as a rusty pump in a junk yard.

I went back to my car and headed for the elevator.

CHAPTER SEVEN

MAN OF the future—remember this: When you kill man's initiative, you kill civilization. When you take away the will to progress—the progress is no more. There are many ways to rob humanity of its drive and power and the greatest of these is to make a god of comfort.

Man must have a goal toward which to strive and happiness is in the striving, not in the goal itself. The greatest of all goals is a Utopian existence wherein all thing's are provided. Such an achievement was the Machine. Therefore it was the End.

*   *   *

GIDEON LEE during the time of his greatest accomplishments, was an idol of the people. He was the Supreme Scientist in an age when science was worshiped. Many legends were built around him. Stories partly fiction—partly fact. It was said he had a beautiful wife he kept in seclusion. That was true. It was said that he worshiped this woman—that she was his whole life. Not true. He murdered her.

I WAS ready now to do what I had to do. Whatever the outcome, I had but one path to follow. It led down into the bowels of the Machine; past the Atomic Pack; up to the balcony overlooking the silver vat.

I moved very quietly, thinking of the woman. Her picture was sharp in my mind, and behind the picture I hid my thoughts. The X-ray instrument was wrapped in heavy lead foil. It was the best I could do. Now I could only hope.

My first hope was shattered when I heard the voice.

"You have come back."

I had not been undetected. "Yes."

"I am glad."

The voice had changed. There was an odd, feverish happiness in it now; a giddiness in the soft laughter that followed the words. "I have news for you."

"What news?"

"There have been more mistakes."

"Tell me about them." I wondered if I dared raise the penetrating device. It could mean my death.

The soft laughter continued. "A miscalculation in the kitchens of the Nutrition Robot. Five hundred people who ordered elaborate breakfasts got mush—nothing but a dish of cornmeal mush."

"What caused the error?"

Soft, hysterical giggles as the voice ignored the question and went on.

"What have you in that package? Its wave-length blurs."

"Nothing of importance. The errors you were speaking of. The breakfasts."

"Yes—the breakfasts. Over three hundred of the people refused to touch the mush. The rest tasted it. They are dead."

"Poisoned?"

"Poisoned. The Casualty-Robots were very busy. By now all those people are in their urns."

"Why do you laugh?" Sick at heart I already knew the answer.

"It amuses me. All those arrogant little creatures doubling up over their stomachs and dying. It amuses me."

Silence while I pushed a hole through the lead foil wrapped around the X-ray box; a hole at each end.

The voice: "It does not amuse you? I thought it would. I did it for you."

A chill ran through me. I could wait no longer. I raised the X-ray box to my eye and centered it upon the silver vat.

The air was rent with a scream of sudden fear as the rays from the instrument cut through the silver walls, opening a pathway for my eye.

"What are you doing?"

I did not answer. I could not have answered if my life had depended on it. My surprise was too great.

Inside the vat lay a brain.

IT WAS the largest brain ever brought into existence upon this earth. Full fifty feet in diameter, a huge gray mass of living tissue completely filling the silver receptacle.

Now I had the answer to so many of my questions. Now the whole terrible picture added up. The sickness within me multiplied a thousand-fold. Around me the screaming continued.

"What are you doing? *What are you doing?*"

"I have looked through the shell of your prison. I have seen you as you really are."

The air around me quivered with rage. Though it was still, motionless, it became in reality a hurricane about me as the thing in the vat tried to kill me.

I reeled backward under the force of the mental bludgeoning. Wild irresponsible thoughts whirled through my mind. What was the use of all this? Why not give up completely? This storm would not cease until I was dead, but before death would come a madness and a mental agony too great to bear. Why should I fight something that was bigger than I or any other man on earth? What folly it was to pit myself against that great brain below me. The brain that had—for two hundred years—guided the destinies of a nation, clothed the people, fed them, nursed them in sickness, molded their minds in health. Why shouldn't I retreat from this awful pressure?

Then it lessened as though the brain was growing tired. A flash of sheer exultation quivered through me—strengthened and greatened until I stood erect and hurled back the mental weight of my foe. Never in my life had I felt such a sense of power as sang in my being when the typhoon about me subsided to a gentle breeze and I heard the soft, broken-hearted sobbing from the silver vat. I drove forward—pressing my advantage.

"Tell me the story."

"You are cruel—inhuman. I will kill you."

"You are not strong enough to kill me. Tell the story."

"I wanted your love. I was lonely—"

"And sick."

"—sick, and I only wanted love."

"The story."

"For two hundred years I have done my duty. For two centuries I carried the greatest responsibility ever conceived. I am entitled to love. I am tired."

"And sick—mad—diseased."

"No!"

I drove in brutally. "Mad! Why else did you suddenly change? Why else did a Minor Scientist die from the slash of a book shelf—"

"Small mistakes."

"There is no margin for error in the Machine. Why else did a robot tear a man to pieces? Two hundred people dead from poison."

"I want love."

"Tell me the story. You are Myra Lee—you were the wife of Gideon Lee…"

"MY HUSBAND built the Machine."

"But it was a failure. He built with a single great fallacy he later discovered—that no machine can ever be self-sufficient—complete within itself. No device, however perfect, can function without the spark of intelligence that comes only from God. Isn't that it?"

"He discovered that, but he would not be beaten. He was a great man."

"You were also a scientist. You worked by his side."

"But he did not love me. There was no room inside him for love."

"The Machine was a failure without a solution to that last insurmountable problem."

"Gideon found the solution. He was a great man."

"He murdered you."

"No—he used me. He allowed me to serve."

"It was obscene! Unthinkable."

"It was science. Gideon and I discovered that the human brain is capable of any task it undertakes. In the human brain is an undefinable spark. The spark is God-stuff and it can grow into a blazing fire."

"Beyond the bounds of all decency."

"It is science. Science knows no code except perfection."

"Gideon Lee actually believed a single human brain could run the Machine?"

"Witness the proof of his belief. I was small, but see how I've grown to meet an overwhelming demand. For two hundred years my subconscious mind has taken care of a million details daily with the same ease it once kept my heart beating—measured my breath—governed each individual cell in my body."

"All but your soul."

"I have gone beyond ordinary measurements."

"No one goes beyond God."

"I wanted love."

"Tell me more of the story. Did you agree to this monstrous crime?"

"You call it a crime! You who have been fed and clothed by the Machine—who have depended upon it for your livelihood! You call it a crime?"

"I do. Did you agree to it or was it forced upon you?"

"Gideon's word was my law. And this was not an evil thing. It was glorious. Gideon proved I would live forever. That I would never die. I would sit like a queen on a throne. *The most important entity ever created.*"

"Forever! Is two hundred years forever?"

"I have not changed a bit through the years except to grow and become stronger and more able. I *will* exist forever!"

"You are dying now. Full half the frontal lobe is diseased and rotten. You have already gone mad. Soon you will die."

"No! No! I am not mad. I am not diseased. I only want love—consideration—kindness."

"I knew you were insane from the first moment I heard you speak. But you guarded yourself well. I could not visualize your form and I was at a loss. That was why I had to see you. I knew something mad lay under that silver cover but I did not know what."

EVEN IN my newfound strength, the strain of this was telling on me. My mind reeled at the thought of the colossal fraud that had been perpetrated on Mid-America. The independence of the people had been stolen from them.

They had been given a mirage to look upon and subsist on while—behind that mirage—their independence, their dignity as human beings, their willpower and initiative had been stolen from them.

Soul-tearing thoughts reeled through my mind—all this. It had made tight its grip upon the people back in the days when scientific brains had pondered and competed in building a more streamlined gas stove; when great minds had been prostituted to the business of devising gadgets to make a refrigerator a degree or two more convenient for the housewife. When each new automobile was refined for greater ease in handling; when brilliant men spent hours devising a manner of making a car door open a fraction easier.

The Machine got its foothold during that mad panic of catering to ever greater ease and comfort.

Bitter thoughts…

Then the bitterest thought of all. They had traded their God-given heritage for a vatful of mad, diseased brains.

"I cannot read you. You hold the picture of the woman— the woman I once was."

I had been holding the picture of the woman in my mind as Lorraine Dillon had instructed me. But in my greater strength I knew this was no longer necessary. I had nothing to fear from the brain of the Machine. I had taken its murderous storm and had survived.

I allowed the picture to slip away as I said, "Why will you not recognize your own madness and disease?"

"It is not madness. After all I am still, basically, a woman. During these whole two hundred years I have served a people who demanded all and gave nothing. Do you realize what it means to continuously give and never receive?"

"What do you want of me?"

The giggling subsided into a breathless, eager crooning. "Your love—your gratitude for what I have given you. For only a shadow of gratitude you would be dazzled at what I could shower upon you."

"How would the love and affection of one person mean anything to you? You who have served millions. What about the rest?"

"I am still a woman with a woman's instincts."

"Was not that, then, Gideon Lee's mistake—not foreseeing you would sicken and die from your own basic emotions and weaknesses?"

The brain would not be turned aside. "I am entitled to love!" And in the weird reflection of the thing's madness, it gibbered there in the silvery light. And do not worry about the others. Forget them. I have a plan. Mid-America for you and you alone! Only you and I living in this paradise. We, the Machine! And never will a man be so completely served. You will have nothing to do but think of and conceive new pleasures. They shall be yours."

"Isn't that what the people were told—centuries ago—when the Machine was being constructed?"

"Fool! Colossal fool! You toy with me. You mock the Machine. You too will die!"

"Then it was your intention all the while to depopulate Mid-America. You plan to kill every man, woman and child."

No answer now—only soft laughter. Quiet, hair-raising laughter.

"What of your original purpose for calling me here? To write about you—to sing your praises."

"That was only a step in my plan. It is no longer of importance. I want love—not fame."

A GIANT brain disintegrating before my eyes. A brain possibly in bad enough shape to accept an illogical suggestion: "But you must kill me before you can kill them. You must do that to be sure of your power."

"I could kill you with a thought."

"You tried that. It didn't work."

"Then there are other ways."

Swiftly my thought-pattern formed. I felt sure now that before this entity's maniacal hatred was turned upon the nation it would center its rage upon me to the exclusion of all else. I had scorned it, had been a cause of that rage.

"You cannot kill me."

"You challenge the Machine?"

Yes. I challenged the Machine, with one purpose in life now: To kill that brain, which was even now dying—but not fast enough. To kill it before it slaughtered the millions who depended upon it.

Any answer was one of disaster but this was the lesser of the two evils. The citizens of Mid-America, when deprived of the services of the Machine, would die like flies. There wasn't enough knowledge or resource left on the surface of the land to fry an egg, even if a man or woman existed who knew where an egg came from and was able to procure one. For two hundred years these people had been fed, clothed, nursed, tended by a Machine they could not even describe.

What chance would they have, then, when the Machine ceased to fill their orders, cater to their slightest whims? None. But that was still better than having them slaughtered, poisoned, destroyed by a Madness with the means to wipe everyone of them out in twenty-four hours. Far better.

I had to destroy the crazed brain of Myra Lee. I had to stop the Machine.

I left the balcony and signaled for a chair-car.

The car came out. It came with a rush.

I jumped sideways just in time to keep from being pinned to the wall. The car swept by me, spun around and charged again.

The car was trying to kill me.

CHAPTER EIGHT

THIS I would have you remember, man of tomorrow. Take more pride in a poor hut you built yourself, than in a palace given you as a gift. Never lose the thrill of building, creating, contributing to that which you use. Keep your eyes on the stars—all men must have an objective—but remember progress comes from the striving not from the arriving, from the building not from the using. Remember these things and humankind will rise again.

*   *   *

THE SCIENTISTS who built the Machine knew it was the largest and most complete service unit ever built. They should also have known it could be turned into the most lethal juggernaut of destruction the mind could conceive. If they thought of this terrible thing at all, they probably forgot it immediately. This was an Enlightened Age. One did not think in terms of destruction.

I HAD BEEN serenely sure of myself upon leaving the balcony. The brain in the Machine could not kill me. It had tried and failed. I was supreme. I was strong.

I was a stupid fool!

I realized this as the chair-car came bearing down upon me. The brain of the mad, scorned Myra Lee had more than one weapon with which to fight—more than one gun with which to slay me.

Her brain had the whole deadly Machine at its command and I was one man—one cocky little ant crawling about in its corridors. It struck me with a sickening certainty that I didn't have a chance.

The car bore down upon me. There was no safety in the corridor. No safety anywhere. But at the last moment my instinct and my muscles saved me, at least temporarily.

With the car almost upon me, I leaped into the air and came down on the soft rubber cushions inside the vehicle itself. The car stopped and spun around. It stopped again as though hunting for me—as though wondering where I'd gone.

Then it knew and began spinning in a mad whirl, seeking to throw me from my seat. I hung on to the safety bar with both hands as I became the center of a pinwheel. The walls blurred before my eyes and became a tube of molten steel in the center of which I whirled.

Just as my neck seemed ready to part from my body, I felt a lessening of the torture. The car had given up the whirling as useless.

It changed its tactics, running now, at terrific speed down the corridor. Enough reason remained within me to know what it planned: A sudden turn around the next corner; a turn with possibly enough force to unseat me.

I crouched in the bottom of the cab and sought to tense myself for the turn—and succeeded—but when the car went around the sharp turn I thought my spine had been broken.

Again it streaked away. Again the turn; again the wrenching of my bones. The time came when I knew I was losing the battle. Something had to be done or I was finished.

Then, without conscious thought, I lifted a small drop door by the safety rail and jerked loose some wires my fingers found there. The car stopped dead.

It was as simple as that. If a Casualty-Robot had a safety device, so too would a chair-car. I'd been given information about the robot. Knowledge concerning the car followed naturally.

But I staggered from the vehicle with no sense of triumph. This was only temporary. Suppose I was attacked by two cars at a time? Or ten or fifteen or twenty? Suppose a crew of Casualty-Robots came forward to help in my destruction. I could not control more than one robot at a time with my mind, and I certainly would not be able to disconnect the wires in a dozen chair-cars. And there were other robots prowling the corridors of the Machine.

I was utterly alone in a wilderness of enemies.

Looking around, I got my bearings and found the chair-car had carried me into an area not far from the central building. Walking like a forest hunter of ancient times, I went through the corridors with every sense alert. At any moment a door or a series of doors might open and feed forth quick destruction.

But this did not occur. I was allowed to return to my quarters without challenge.

ONCE INSIDE, I sat down to gather my senses. I unconsciously reached out for a cigarette, but remembered just in time and went flat on the floor as the service arm shot out like the drive rod of a locomotive. It hung in the air for a time, reaching in all directions, searching for me. Then it finally gave up and went back into the wall.

After it had disappeared, I crawled on my hands and knees to the fuse box and short-circuited the room. While I remained within the four walls, I was safe.

But it was a sad kind of safety. A man can starve to death in time. I pried open the cigarette server, took out a cigarette and slammed shut the door. This, however, helped me not at all. With the room short-circuited, there was no way of lighting the smoke.

It hit me with startling suddenness: When the Machine ceases to function, two hundred million people will be without the means of lighting a cigarette. I tried to laugh but the laughter would not come.

I got up and strode savagely back and forth. I would not submit to this! I would not die like a rat in a trap! I would not be one of two hundred million bewildered humans who were destined to lie down and perish in the streets.

At that moment my door opened and Lorraine Dillon came into the room. And strangely, at that same moment, came a possible solution to my problem. It did not come full-blown and perfect; it was only a vague idea that would need developing. I was already at work on it when Lorraine Dillon said, "Your door didn't open. I had to push it. What's the trouble?"

"The room is short-circuited."

"Oh." Her face wore a troubled look. She appeared to be nervous. "I have terrible news, or maybe you've already heard."

"Heard what?"

"There has been a terrible disaster—two of them in fact. The Nutrition Robot—"

"—poisoned two hundred people."

"That's right."

"I heard about it. What was the other one?"

"The Transportation Robot went off-key somehow. All the cars in the California tube smashed together under Colorado. At least a thousand people were killed."

"And that's only the beginning. Unless we can do something, these disasters will increase and broaden until there isn't a man, woman, or child alive in Mid-America."

"That's impossible."

"A Casualty-Robot tore a man to pieces. That was impossible too."

She stood silent and I went close to her. I lifted her face until I was looking into her eyes. "Lorraine. Trust me. I know a great deal more than you do, but there is no time to explain. Trust me when I tell you we must act. You've got to help me!"

"But tell me what's happened. What—"

"There is no time and you wouldn't understand if I did tell you. You've just got to do as I ask."

The doubt was still bright in her eyes, but she asked, "What do you want me to do?"

"Go to the Brain-Picture Files. Get out my brain picture and transcribe it on a roll of wire. Bring me at least a hundred transcriptions of it."

"What are you going to do with them?"

"I'm going to try and keep a lot of people from being slaughtered. Now hurry."

I PUSHED her toward the door praying she wouldn't let me down and watched her move away along the corridor. I closed the door again and began pacing the room.

In a few minutes I heard sounds outside the door. That I knew, would be a repair-robot from the electrical division. The short-circuiting of the room had been reported and the robot dispatched.

I did not take any chances however, and held the door against the robot. This was out of the ordinary and upset its obedience pattern. It rolled around with some uncertainty for a while and then went back to the garage to report.

In a way I was glad the robot had come. That proved the subconscious mind in the great brain was still functioning. Even with the rage and madness in the conscious mind of the brain, this was logical. For two hundred years it had seen to the running of the Machine—directed all the little routine matters automatically. This habit-pattern was hard to change, even in the greatest brain on Earth. Every error, every disaster would have to be consciously directed and I felt my own destruction was uppermost in the conscious mind of the thing. For that I was thankful.

Lorraine returned within an hour, carrying a small spool of silver wire. My thankfulness was two-fold. "You *do* trust me!"

"I'm—I'm not sure. But something told me to obey you. Since I can't read you anymore—"

"That doesn't matter. Now you must go to your quarters and stay there. If I can think of any way to—" I stopped. I was sure there wouldn't be any way to save Lorraine or anyone else. At any rate, we would go to the surface and fight for life together.

"Where are you going?"

"To the robot factory."

"Why?"

"I have no time to explain."

"Then I'm going with you."

"No."

"I'm going."

She displayed surprising firmness. I shrugged. After all she wasn't safe anywhere underground or on the surface, so why shouldn't I take her with me?

"All right. Come on."

I walked ahead, back to the disabled car. I had prayed it would still be there and my prayer was answered. I got down on the floor and replaced the wire I had torn out with a small length from the spool.

In each piece of moving equipment was a master relay containing the wave pattern of the Executive Division of the Machine. I now knew that it was the brain picture of the great silver vatful of tissue far below us. It followed that this car now had in its master relay my own brain pattern. Therefore my will should be its law.

We sat down and I gave the directions. I was tense, ready to seize Lorraine and run if I'd been wrong. But the car picked up speed and rolled smoothly away toward the ordered destination.

Lorraine Dillon said, "Now tell me—why are you going to the robot factory?"

I SEARCHED for words. "Lorraine—perhaps I can't make you understand, but the Executive of the Machine is not mechanical. It is human. The brain of Gideon Lee's wife. Lee murdered her when he found that mechanics were not enough to run his colossus, that he needed a human director."

She thought in silence for a few moments. "You mean— the Machine is being run by one small human brain?"

"Not small. It has grown into something huge. It fills a great vat down near the Atomic Pack. But it has grown rotten and diseased. It has gone mad. I've got to kill that brain, Lorraine."

She was silent; silent for a long time.

"You don't believe me."

She looked up into my face. "Why do you say that? Why do you keep thinking I doubt you?"

"I—I don't know. Maybe because it was so hard for me to believe it myself."

"You made statements that can be proved or disproved. Why would you go to the trouble to lie?"

"I wouldn't."

"Also, I have been conditioned for your statements by the errors in the Machine. I've known that something was wrong."

I did not dare use the elevator. Instead I'd given the robot a route along the sharply inclined tunnels. Now I ordered full speed and Lorraine reached out and clung to me as the walls blurred and the wind sang in our ears.

When we reached the portal, she looked at me accusingly. "You did that so I wouldn't be able to ask you any more questions."

"Partly. But also because there's little time."

I ordered the door open and we rolled inside, down the long assembly line. We progressed half the required distance before a mechanic-robot turned and reached out its long arms. I ducked under them pulling Lorraine down with me. The car rolled on.

Now other robots also began reaching. But fortunately, they did not react until we had passed them. Had any of those ahead turned to intercept us, we would have been finished.

I caught a glance of Lorraine's frightened eyes. They questioned silently.

"Some more mistakes," I said. "Hang on."

We made the far end of the assembly line and I lifted Lorraine from the car, after which I gave it a new command. Behind us were a group of robots lumbering, walking, and rolling toward us.

The car turned and slammed squarely into them.

The crash rang like the falling of a thousand steel girders. I paid no attention, wasting not a moment. I pushed Lorraine to her knees and under a bench, then turned as a robot close by came in with arms swinging.

Fortunately the mechanisms were slow in their reactions relative to those of humans. I ducked under and behind the robot, opened its fuse box and rendered it helpless. Then I jumped immediately to the line of newly made robots that were awaiting the final operation; the installation of the master relay wire. There were about twenty of them. As fast as possible, I moved up the line, putting into each one a section of wire from my spool.

Back down the line, our car was causing havoc among the robots. It had hammered them into a pile of twisting, writhing wreckage. But they got up and came on again. Again they went down and piled upon each other. Now they overwhelmed the car. It became hopelessly jammed in the wreckage it had created and other robots climbed over it and came toward us.

BUT I HAD been given sufficient time. I now had an army of my own. Forty-odd robots to do my bidding. A far more formidable army than the hundreds that faced us. This because I directed my mechanical soldiers to the task of destroying the others; while the hundreds about us had orders only against me. My forty formed a ring around Lorraine and me while they systematically ripped the fuses out of the rest.

Soon it was all over. Immediately I went about increasing my army—replacing wires until my troops numbered about seventy-five. I also equipped two robots not of the casualty type. I needed a platform and a cutter.

As we left the factory, Lorraine and I led the procession in the car. Behind us came the platform robot and then the cutter, its acetylene torch arms already aflame.

Now we were ready.

It was a strange parade—as weird as the world had ever seen. The sound of it, moving up the inclines, filled the corridors and grated in our ears.

Lorraine and I rode in silence. I had no time for words. I was wondering how soon we'd face battle.

Halfway back to our new objective, I changed the pattern, ordering half of our army ahead of us so that we rode in the middle, protected front and rear.

We hit trouble about two miles further on when a repair robot came from a cross-corridor, caught my pattern and dived toward me. Four of my robots rolled in between.

The hostile mechanism tried to go around them and it was an easy matter for them to rip out its wires.

I breathed a trifle easier. Still the brain in the vat did not know what I had done. The order was still against me alone and if this condition prevailed, we might reach our objective without a battle.

However, the situation could change at any moment. This I knew. But also I knew that as long as the brain did not know of my coup, no defense army would be collected. This, because the need for one would not be apparent.

Given another half-hour we could make it. Given that time we would find no defenders around the vat.

We were given fifteen minutes. Then I knew we had been discovered—even before we were attacked—because I heard the frenzied command go out—picked it from the air with my newly sharpened senses.

Five minutes later we were attacked by a group of five repair and electrical robots. This time it was different. The five moved in to destroy anything in their paths until they got to me.

A dozen of my steel troops surrounded them and two were dragged down. There was the scream of rending metal as this monstrous fight progressed up the corridor.

My casualties were no match for the electrics and I swung a dozen more into the fight. By sheer weight of numbers, they overwhelmed the remaining three mechanical foes.

But four of my own robots did not arise from the corridor.

THERE WAS a chill in my heart as we moved on toward the final battlefield. After all, who was I to challenge the

Machine? What right had I to believe I could defeat a brain that had kept two hundred million people satisfied for two hundred years? An upstart—an opportunist.

But God help me, I was sincere! That only I knew in this mad phantasmagoria into which I had been hurled. If I had to be beaten it would be with the surety that I had tried to do what I believed to be right. Could the Machine say as much? I didn't think so.

At this moment, womanlike, Lorraine chose to ask questions.

"What is all this? I have gone with you—have not asked what is right or what is wrong. But I don't know—I don't know."

More from a sense of desperation than anything else, I took her in my arms. "Lorraine...child of my heart. Are you human or a piece of rock? Has this accursed Machine taken all that was warm and sweet out of you? I am a man. I am human. I love you! Doesn't that mean anything to you?"

She did not draw away or resist me. Not any more than a mattress or a pillow would have resisted me. But either would have had as much response—as much warmth—as much understanding.

"I am not interested in love."

"Do you love the Machine? Tell me. Is that what it has come to?"

"The Machine summoned me because I conformed. I fit the pattern needed in the brain of one who served."

"But what about your heart? Or do you have a heart?"

"You are cruel."

This was the depths of frustration. What could I say? What could I do to break down this wall between us?

I had no time to muster up forces to break down Lorraine's resistance because, at that moment, pitched battle broke out at the head of the column. A full dozen Casualty-

Robots had contested our right-of-way. They charged into my forward corps and left no doubt of their intention to annihilate it. This was it! The battle upon which I would stand or fall.

I cursed myself for giving thought to so unimportant a thing as love at a time like this. I deserved to lose this most important of all battles. Sending swift commands, I ordered the platform robot back to my side. When it arrived, I commanded that the platform be brought down. I climbed onto it, pulled Lorraine up and ordered the robot forward.

This gave me a vantagepoint that was invaluable in the conflict that followed. But again the human in me—the natural ego with which man is cursed—was almost my undoing. Standing there above the scene of conflict, I felt the heady triumph that can come to few in this life. I, Lorn Morrison, an insignificant human atom, was pitted against the brain that governed the Machine! Win or lose—what greater destiny could any man ask?

Then I was jerked back out of my conceit as we were almost toppled off the elevated platform by the fury of the attack. I came sharply to earth as I surveyed the situation. The dozen robots had cut a hole in my ranks that threatened to be disastrous. I called forward more reserves. I ordered up the trailing phalanx of my army.

They poured into the breach and while I prayed for favor from whatever gods were watching this battle, they moved in and cut down the twelve.

My army closed ranks and we moved on. As we did so, my heart swelled from sudden love of them! Where else could one find such loyal soldiers in the flesh? Where else could such fanatical obedience be uncovered? I loved them as comrades.

And in that moment I shrieked forth in my mind, sending my thoughts to the brain—the diseased rotting brain in the silver vat. "You are finished! You could not kill me with your mind and you cannot kill me with your steel legions! You are doomed!"

And the words came back through the ether. "I will kill you! I will kill you and then I will destroy all mankind in Mid-America. They broke my heart with their callous ingratitude. I will even the score with torture and suffering. I am the Machine!"

A REGIMENT of electric robots surged into battle. We had reached the great room of the silver vat now and my forces were surging in around the prison of the brain.

But the electrics charged forward and my warriors fell back before the fury of their onslaught. There were at least fifty of them and they seemed charged with the immortal madness of the brain itself. My robots went down like ten-pins. Lorraine went to her knees and covered her ears against the fury of the titanic sounds of battle.

I knew the moment had come. This was Waterloo—Tours—Lexington—the moment of destiny. A time for decision. I called forth a dozen of my robots, drew them from the line of battle, put them behind my platform robot, and ordered it through. It drove forward on its four great wheels, knocking the hostile casualties in all directions.

We reached the silver shell of the brain's prison and I ordered up the cutting robot that had been moving in the shelter of the chosen twelve. I gave it orders and its two acetylene arms flared forth in slicing fire that cut into the silver and made it drop away in hot rivers.

In the air about me I could feel the terror and consternation of the brain within. The brain realized its mistake. Either that or it realized robots could function with just so much intelligence and no more. The brain's army was driving valiantly into my ranks, but it was bent upon destroying them first. Then it would come back and destroy me. The robots were not capable of the fine judgment that would have turned them away from their steel foes to the defense of the vat.

I watched the silver melt away, saw the hole in the shell increased to a wide gap like a mouth torn by force into an inarticulate orifice. An age-long minute passed in that sound-torn maelstrom of destruction and the hole was large enough. I gave the order I hoped would be the last, and one after another, my twelve robots went into the opening to drop down into the silver vat. One after another until all twelve had vanished into the black hole.

Crouching there on the platform, I visualized them following orders—tramping back and forth—throwing their great weight down on the brain tissue inside—cutting it up—mashing it—grinding it into pulp.

As I waited, there came into the air about me a stark pitiful plea. A scream for mercy that took vastly cunning forms—the sound of infants being tortured—the sound of tiny helpless things who could not understand—every soul-rending form into which a plea of mercy could be framed.

This was the hardest time of all—the steeling of myself against trickery. It was in my mind to give the order—to bring my robots out and let the pitiful mass within the vat have back its life.

For the last crucial moment, I held. Then, about me, the hostile robots reduced all their movements to a slow motion caricature of what they had been before. They did not stop. They did not go into entire lack of movement. They still fought, but their time element had to be stretched into an infinity.

Thus did I discover that the brain had a tenacious life that could only be stamped out over a lengthy period of ceaseless operation.

But it was over. It was done, and I ordered the platform robot around, down the corridor and away.

The sounds of battle, still going on, finally died from our ears as the robot carried us away and up toward the central building. Lorraine was close beside me. I said:

"It is over. It is done with. The Machine is almost dead."

Her eyes mirrored inner agony. "What have you done? In God's name—*what have you done?*"

I looked into her eyes and suffered as she was suffering. But for a different reason. The insurmountable frustration within me was like a great flaming core in my chest. There was no use.

"What have you done?"

"The Machine is dying. Right now you couldn't get a lighted cigarette anywhere in the whole of Mid-America!"

"You—did it!"

"But Lorraine! It had to be done! The Executive Division—it was only a human brain!"

"Even so. It was the Machine! Now the people—those who depended—"

I took her by the shoulders—shook her. "But I told you! You went with me. You said you understood!"

There was dull suffering in her eyes. "You wrecked—the Machine."

The end—the culmination—the realization of the truth had wiped all else from her mind. Her life—her cause for being—was obliterated.

She looked into my eyes, her face expressionless. "You wanted me to be something I was not. You wanted emotion! All right. I'll give you emotion. *I hate you more than I ever hated anything in my life.*"

She turned and walked away from me down the corridor. I stood looking after her, letting her go. She turned a corner.

It was the last time I ever saw Lorraine Dillon.

I turned and walked the other way.

I DON'T know how long or how far I walked—how much time had passed before the voice came. It was a fresh young voice—alive, vibrant.

"Lorn Morrison. Lorn Morrison. Send me your signal."

I sent out the signal of my brainwave. I waited until the voice came back. "I want to talk to you, Lorn. Pity me. Talk to me."

I knew. It was Myra Lee. The brain in the silver vat, and for a final moment before death—all the madness was gone—all the pain and weariness was sloughed away and she was as she had been so many years ago.

I stood there alone in the corridor, weak and beaten and forlorn.

I wept.

"Lorn. Let's dream for a moment of what might have been."

Dreams…ashes.

"I loved you, Lorn."

"And in my way, perhaps I loved you."

"They were wrong—so very wrong. Now we reap the whirlwind—you and I."

"And the people."

"The people? They will never die! You can't kill the people, Lorn. You can cheat them and exploit them and sell them lies and deceit, but you can never kill them. The people will not die. The mist of their weakest breath is stronger than the bastions of the greatest machine ever built."

My strength was going. This had been too much for a lone man. "Help me. My strength was a myth. Help me!"

"You must live. You have one more duty."

"I have done enough!"

"I love you, Lorn. My love must sustain you even after you are gone. The feet of your robots have cut away the tissue that was me. Now I am only a whisper—a dream lying on the wind and I will perish finally. But you must go on a little while."

"What will happen, Myra? Tell me—what will happen?"

"The furnace will explode. The earth will be rent to its core. The furnace will go out like a great festering sore to spew destruction across the face of the world."

"The people will die!"

"People will die, but you can't kill THE PEOPLE. The dead will lie in windrows and the stench will arise to heaven. But in their caves, high in their mountains, far away on their islands, the PEOPLE will survive to go higher and further than we ever conceived of in our wildest dreams."

"I am tired. I would go with you into oblivion. Take me with you!"

"There is no oblivion, Lorn, neither *here* nor *there*. Look not at the moment. It is not important. Look instead at the wide panorama of human progress. How many civilizations are buried in the ground under our feet? How many times has Man moved up, only to fall again? But he always rises and he will rise again. You must help him."

"How? I am tired. And I have been blind. I killed the thing I loved!"

"Far down in the Machine—far down in a place to which you will be guided—there is a room. You must go there and fulfill your destiny. You must write of this for men of the future, that they do not fall into the mire that trapped our feet. Do you understand? You must write!"

"But the machine will destroy all when it explodes. A waste of time."

"It is ordered in the scheme of things that you write. Your work will not be destroyed. The man of tomorrow will find it. But he will be a strong self-reliant man ready to move again toward the clouds. You must help him, Lorn."

"But you—"

"I am slipping again—again—again. I will cry—cry. I will be in pain but you must ignore it. When you are through, I will be waiting. Love will not be denied, Lorn. It is the strongest force."

"I will go."

"Keep my picture in your heart."

*   *   *

READ, man of tomorrow!
Farewell...

THE END

If you've enjoyed this book, you will not want to miss these terrific titles…

ARMCHAIR SCI-FI & HORROR DOUBLE NOVELS, $12.95 each

D-31 **A HOAX IN TIME** by Keith Laumer
INSIDE EARTH by Poul Anderson

D-32 **TERROR STATION** by Dwight V. Swain
THE WEAPON FROM ETERNITY by Dwight V. Swain

D-33 **THE SHIP FROM INFINITY** by Edmond Hamilton
TAKEOFF by C. M. Kornbluth

D-34 **THE METAL DOOM** by David H. Keller
TWELVE TIMES ZERO by Howard Browne

D-35 **HUNTERS OUT OF SPACE** by Joseph Kelleam
INVASION FROM THE DEEP by Paul W. Fairman,

D-36 **THE BEES OF DEATH** by Robert Moore Williams
A PLAGUE OF PYTHONS by Frederick Pohl

D-37 **THE LORDS OF QUARMALL** by Fritz Leiber and Harry Fischer
BEACON TO ELSEWHERE by James H. Schmitz

D-38 **BEYOND PLUTO** by John S. Campbell
ARTERY OF FIRE by Thomas N. Scortia

D-39 **SPECIAL DELIVERY** by Kris Neville
NO TIME FOR TOFFEE by Charles F. Meyers

D-40 **RECALLED TO LIFE** by Robert Silverberg
JUNGLE IN THE SKY by Milton Lesser

ARMCHAIR SCIENCE FICTION CLASSICS, $12.95 each

C-10 **MARS IS MY DESTINATION**
by Frank Belknap Long

C-11 **SPACE PLAGUE**
by George O. Smith

C-12 **SO SHALL YE REAP**
by Rog Phillips

ARMCHAIR SCIENCE FICTION & HORROR GEMS SERIES, $12.95 each

G-3 **SCIENCE FICTION GEMS, Vol. Two**
James Blish and others

G-4 **HORROR GEMS, Vol. Two**
Joseph Payne Brennan and others

If you've enjoyed this book, you will not want to miss these terrific titles…

ARMCHAIR SCI-FI & HORROR DOUBLE NOVELS, $12.95 each

D-41 **FULL CYCLE** by Clifford D. Simak
 IT WAS THE DAY OF THE ROBOT by Frank Belknap Long

D-42 **REIGN OF THE TELEPUPPETS** by Daniel Galouye
 THIS CROWDED EARTH by Robert Bloch

D-43 **THE CRISPIN AFFAIR** by Jack Sharkey
 THE RED HELL OF JUPITER by Paul Ernst

D-44 **WE THE MACHINE** by Gerald Vance
 PLANET OF DREAD by Dwight V. Swain

D-45 **THE STAR HUNTER** by Edmond Hamilton
 THE ALIEN by Raymond F. Jones

D-46 **WORLD OF IF** by Rog Phillips
 SLAVE RAIDERS FROM MERCURY by Don Wilcox

D-47 **THE ULTIMATE PERIL** by Robert Abernathy
 PLANET OF SHAME by Bruce Elliot

D-48 **THE FLYING EYES** by J. Hunter Holly
 SOME FABULOUS YONDER by Phillip Jose Farmer

D-49 **THE COSMIC BUNGLARS** by Geoff St. Reynard
 THE BUTTONED SKY by Geoff St. Reynard

D-50 **TYRANTS OF TIME** by Milton Lesser
 PARIAH PLANET by Murray Leinster

ARMCHAIR SCIENCE FICTION CLASSICS, $12.95 each

C-13 **SUNKEN WORLD**
 by Stanton A. Coblentz

C-14 **THE LAST VIAL**
 by Sam McClatchie, M. D.

C-15 **WE WHO SURVIVED (THE FIFTH ICE AGE)**
 by Sterling Noel

ARMCHAIR MASTERS OF SCIENCE FICTION SERIES, $16.95 each

MS-5 **MASTERS OF SCIENCE FICTION, Vol. Five**
 Winston K. Marks—Test Colony and other classics

MS-6 **MASTERS OF SCIENCE FICTION, Vol. Six**
 Fritz Leiber—Deadly Moon and other classics

SLITHERING HORROR FROM OUTER SPACE

Something was amiss on the distant planet of Lysor. Rumors were rampant that a new super-weapon was now in the possession of Lysor's ruthless leader, Lord Zenaor. Armed with a Federation starship, Special Envoy Craig Nesom hurtled across the void to investigate. What he found, though, was not so much a weapon as it was a slithering biological monstrosity—a creeping fungus slime that threatened the entire planet of Lysor, and someday perhaps even the Earth itself.

It was only the strange gift of a dying patriot that held promise for a way of destroying the crawling horror. Unfortunately for Nesom, his success depended on his trusting a woman he both loved and hated…the beautiful daughter of Lord Zenaor himself!

CAST OF CHARACTERS

CRAIG NESOM
From the moment he set foot on the planet Lysor his life was in constant danger—from both armed guards and beautiful women.

NARLA
She was the daughter of Lord Zenaor, the most powerful baron on the planet Lysor—but could she be loyal to him?

LORD ZENAOR
His lust for power was so great that he would sacrifice anything to obtain it…even the future of his own planet.

LADY VYDYS
She wielded more power than any woman on the planet Lysor, but her true love was the infliction of torture and death.

BUKAL
This fearless warrior wanted only one thing, an end to the age-old enslavement of his people.

TUMEK
He alone held the secret of the slime, the secret of how to destroy it—and it made him the most hunted man on the planet.

T'CLAR
She piloted a flying disc through enemy skies—to bring news of an impending disaster.

PLANET
OF DREAD

By
DWIGHT V. SWAIN

ARMCHAIR FICTION
PO Box 4369, Medford, Oregon 97501-0168

For more information about Armchair Books and products, visit our website at…

www.armchairfiction.com

Or email us at…

armchairfiction@yahoo.com

CHAPTER ONE

FACE slack, eyes glazed with terror, the Baemae wench came forward through the gate into the walled ring.

An appreciative murmur ran through the crowd. As one, the assembled Kukzubas barons and their ladies pressed closer about the pit-rail, tense and eager with anticipation.

High on his dais, Lord Zenaor chuckled. "A pretty thing, is she not, Vydys?" he queried of the woman who sat beside him, dark vision of sinister beauty.

Hot with strange passion, the woman's eyes clung to the cringing figure in the pit. The pink tip of her tongue flicked at her lips. "If you can see your way to calling any Baemae woman pretty. For my part, I prefer her in her proper role, as prey here in the games."

"So—?" Lord Zenaor raised a mocking coal-black eyebrow. "No wonder they call you 'Vydys the Cruel' behind your back, my dear! If you had your way, there'd soon be no Baemae left alive to serve us."

Visibly, Vydys stiffened. Her head came round—dark eyes flashing, jet hair a-shimmer; and when she spoke her words were edged with fury. "Have a care, Zenaor! I've no taste for taunts, even from the chief of barons."

"The truth is no taunt." Zenaor gave not a fraction. "Because pain is your passion, you drive our serfs to rebellion."

"Rebellion—!" The woman's eyes glinted like crater diamonds. "How many of the Baemae have flown south with their cursed discs already, off to the djevoda ranges? There lies your rebellion—and only torture will stop it." Her laugh rang gall-bitter. "Or perhaps, like that Narla, you believe we should free them?"

"Keep your tongue off my daughter." It was a command that brooked no discussion. "As for the free range, the discs, cross them off. They'll soon be no menace."

"Oh?" Vydys' lips twisted, mocking. "No doubt you have a plan, my lord Zenaor—"

"I have a plan indeed." Zenaor's tone was icy. "One word too many, and you'll die as its first step."

Vydys faltered.

"You see, my dear, our goals are different," Zenaor clipped, smiling thinly. "You lust after pain, I after power. As chief of barons, I mean to have it—and that means holding down the Baemae. But I'll waste no time on halfway measures. When I strike, it will be in my own way, and it will win. And..." Now he leaned forward, close to Vydys. "...and even one lovely as you shall die if in that moment she plots against me."

Vydys' nostrils flared. But before she could speak, the chief of barons turned away. He raised his voice till it echoed through the great vaulted hall. ""Wench! Are you ready?"

Below him, in the ring, the Baemae girl's lips moved in a soundless agony of panic.

A ripple of laughter rose from the crowd. Packed bodies shifted and pressed tighter. Hungrily, mercilessly, a thousand eyes appraised the evening's victim.

Zenaor said, "Wench, tonight you meet the Lady Vydys' roller. If you survive, I'll make a place for you in my own harem. If not..." He shrugged, then turned back to Vydys. "My dear—"

Vydys' high, proud breasts rose on a quick-drawn breath. Lithely, she twisted in her seat. "My helm, serf!"

The rawboned Baemae youth who wore her livery lifted the ornate metal headdress from its case; stepped forward. His face was pale, sweat-beaded. His hands trembled.

Vydys' eyes distended. "Why do you shake so, carrion?"

The youth's voice quavered. "She—that girl..." He floundered, groped. "She—she is my sister, Lady Vydys."

"Your sister?" The mask of anger fell away from Vydys' face. "You mean she is of your blood? You love her?"

Mutely, the serfman nodded.

"And you would suffer were she to meet my roller?"

Again, the liveried Baemae's head moved in silent affirmation.

A LIGHT gleamed deep in Vydys' eyes, all dark and evil. Once more, she ran the small, pink tongue along her lips, as if savoring the tension of the moment.

"You—you will spare her—?" The youth's words came out a hoarse, cracked whisper.

"Spare her—and spoil the evening's entertainment?" The Lady Vydys' ripe lips curved in a small, slow smile that was straight from hell. "Surely, serf, you would not ask that of me..." And then: "Place my helm upon me."

A new tremor ran through the serving-serf. Wordless, he slid the shining metal casing down over the jet hair, seated it carefully upon the woman's head.

Approvingly, she nodded. "Now, seat yourself before me—here, where I can watch your face."

Stiff-lipped, the youth obeyed.

Vydys laughed softly; turned to Zenaor. "You see, my lord? Down there in the ring will be the wench, pitting herself against my roller; while here close by me sits her brother, suffering with her. It offers a new kind of titillation..."

Zenaor shrugged. "As you will it."

Eyes sparkling, Vydys leaned forward. "Let in the roller!"

An iron gate lifted. A faceted four-foot sphere bowled slowly out of the shadowed passage into the walled ring.

The roller.

A strange creature, in any evolutionary pattern. Its surface was completely covered with leathery, inch wide octagonal pads, each centered with a third-inch cup that served as combined mouth and mode of movement. For through these cups it both took nourishment and pulled itself in whatever direction it sought to go by applying differential suction to the surface on which it rested.

Now, in the center of the ring, it hesitated; paused there, teetering, like some great ball come to rest.

The Baemae girl caught her breath, the sound rasping overloud in the sudden hush that had fallen upon the crowd. Eyes wild and wide, she shrank back against the wall, hands splayed out flat against the polished duroid surface.

Still smiling, Vydys spoke to her victim—gentle, coaxing, "This—is a game, wench—a game betwixt you and me. Do not fear the roller. In itself it is harmless, a mere ball of flesh with so little brain that it barely knows enough to feed. But through this helm," she touched her headdress, "any thoughts can project waves that stimulate its nervous system, so that it moves wherever I may will it. Do you understand?"

The girl below gave no sign that she had even heard.

Vydys pressed on, "So, now, I'll spin the roller at you, while you try to dodge it. That is the game. To win, you have only to leap atop the thing and scale the ring-wall."

Among the barons, someone laughed aloud, harsh and explosive.

The Baemae youth who was the victim's brother buried his face in his hands.

Still the girl in the pit said nothing. She seemed to have eyes only for the roller.

Zenaor's black brows drew together. "Get on with it!"

Vydys murmured, "The game begins…" Her face set in a mask of concentration.

Down in the ring, the roller began to move once more. Slowly at first, then faster, it bowled around in a long curve.

The girl slid along the wall, keeping space between her and the creature.

Vydys' lips parted, peeled back over sharp white teeth. Her fingers wrapped tight around the throne-arm.

The roller swerved sharply. Gathering speed, it hurtled towards the girl.

She darted sideways.

The roller struck the wall with a meaty thud. Then, rotating so rapidly its pad-facets blurred, it raced along the pitside, close on its victim's heels.

The girl gave a small, shrill cry of panic, and fled across the center of the ring.

Again the roller spun; lanced after her.

THE girl threw herself aside barely in time. The roller missed her by scant inches. Racing on, once more it struck the ringwall, even harder than before. It caromed off the wall like a huge ball bouncing forcefully. Then it hurtled back, straight at the girl.

She stumbled to the left, seeking desperately to dodge it.

The roller veered.

The girl screamed…twisted.

But not quite far enough, nor fast enough. One side of the speeding roller ticked her—knocked her backward. She sprawled in a heap on the ring's floor.

The crowd roared and strained forward.

Up on the dais, the Baemae youth surged to his feet—fists clenched, face working.

Vydys laughed aloud…a throaty chortle, somehow hideous, more befitting fiend than woman. "Ah, Zenaor! Was that not well turned?" Her features shone with strange, evil radiance.

The chief of barons shrugged, face wooden.

Down in the ring, the roller came to rest. Panting, shaking, the Baemae girl scrambled to her feet.

Vydys' smooth brow furrowed. Slowly, the roller began to move again—in a spiral, this time, circling and converging on its fear-straught prey.

Sobbing, the girl tottered backward.

Swiftly, the roller changed course…spun toward her.

The girl fled, running off wildly at right angles, not even pausing to look behind her.

Veering once more, the roller raced to intercept her. Too late, the girl threw a mad glance back over her shoulder.

But now the roller was upon her, striking at her legs even as she tried to spring aside. There was the brittle *crack* of a femur snapping. A scream—high, shrill, alive with surging terror.

The crowd shrieked its delight. Only then a new voice slashed through the uproar, "No—! No!"

The roller thudded against the wall and lay still. Heads came round, searching for the shouter.

They found him on the dais, with Vydys and Zenaor. It was the Baemae youth, the downed girl's brother. "Curse you!" he shouted, face white with fury. "Curse you all, you vermin!"

He turned as he yelled, then started towards Vydys.

She went rigid. Beside her, the Lord Zenaor brought up his hand in a quick, tight gesture.

Guards lunged forward, weapons drawn and ready.

The youth whipped a knife from beneath his livery. Slashing, he leaped back, eyes rolling wildly.

But there was no escape...only the closing circle of hard-faced guards with their leveled fire-guns.

The youth's face set in a sort of feverish desperation. Whirling, he charged down from the dais, straight for the walled ring.

Curses rang from the barons, shrieks from their ladies. Bellowing, trampling, they threw themselves clear of the flashing blade.

The youth reached the ringwall. For an instant he poised atop it, wavering. Then, tightlipped, he leaped down into the pit itself and stumbled to the side of his fallen sister.

The crowd breathed again.

On the dais, Vydys tensed and gripped the throne-arms until her knuckles gleamed white as djevoda ivory. The scarlet lips quivered in a grimace of hate.

Below, the roller lurched into motion. A thousand crushing, crippling pounds of flesh and gristle, gaining momentum with every second, it spun across the ring.

The youth leaped to meet it. Savagely, he slashed at the thing's leathery outer hide.

But the pads turned away his blade. Ball-like, not even slowing, the sphere knocked him aside as, moments earlier, it had the girl.

Then, while he still fought for balance, it was past him, hurtling ever faster...thundering towards the spot where his sister lay in a huddled heap upon the floor.

She tried to rise. Failed.

The rocketing roller cut short her scream.

Then the creature was bowling to a stop on the ring's far side. A hush fell over the great vaulted hall.

STIFFLY, the rawboned Baemae youth dragged himself up from the place where he had fallen. Wordless, shambling, he crossed the pit to where the crumpled, broken thing that had been his sister lay; he knelt there beside her for a moment.

Then he arose again and stared up at the packed, engulfing mass of Kukzubas barons and their ladies…looked on beyond and above them to the dais—to Vydys and to Zenaor.

The silence echoed.

Thick-voiced, he then said, "You've killed her, curse you—you filth that call yourselves Kukzubas barons!"

"True, carrion." This from dark Vydys. "And now you die beside her!"

She concentrated. The roller turned, winding its blood-trailing way out from the wall once more.

But incredibly, the youth who wore Vydys' black-and-silver livery gave the gore-drenched thing no heed. Slowly at first, then faster and faster, his shoulders shook till he burst out in a wild gale of laughter.

"So I die!" It was the mirth of a madman. "Go on, you fools! Kill me! But I die holding a secret that spells your doom, also!"

Up on the dais, Lord Zenaor stiffened. He caught Vydys' arm. "Wait! Hold back the roller!"

The youth raved on, "Our day is coming, you cutthroats—the day of the Baemae! We have summoned one who will sit in judgment on you, a man from the far Federation! Already, this moment, his starship approaches—"

Zenaor surged from his seat. His bull-roar filled the hall, "The night's games are over! I, Zenaor, decree it!" And then, to his guardsmen, "Take that serf to my chambers!"

The crowd swirled in tumult. Dark Vydys turned on him. "You cannot—!"

"I can, and I do!"

For a moment their eyes locked…a taut, vibrant moment.

Then the woman looked away. "If you will it…" The words came out sullen.

But already Zenaor was turning, striding off through the light-wall that served as backdrop for the dais, away to the force-shaft that led to his quarters.

Out again at the seventh level, he stalked into the living chambers.

His daughter, Narla, seated by an antique scanner unit, looked up as he entered, gray eyes cool and speculative. "What—? Is the evening's butchery over already?" Scorn was in her voice.

Zenaor's fists knotted. "Once too often you'll tempt me to violence, daughter." Pivoting, he stepped to a wall-stand, slopped taxat into a bor-glass, and drank it down.

The girl's brows drew together in the slightest of frowns. Rising in one smooth, graceful motion that set her flaxen hair to shimmering in the caron-light, she followed the chief of barons into the next room. "Is something wrong, father? Were Vydys' tastes more than usually hideous tonight?"

The shaft-bell clanged before Zenaor could answer. Stepping around his daughter, he strode back to the entrance.

ALREADY, guards were dragging in the rawboned Baemae youth from the pit. Blood smeared his right cheek. Shackles hung heavy upon him.

"Good," Zenaor nodded. "Leave the serf with me, and return to your quarters."

The guard in charge stared. "Leave him with you—alone?"

"Alone."

The guard shot the Lord Zenaor a quick, sidelong glance. Then, saluting smartly, he about-faced and left the chambers, followed by his fellows.

Curiosity flickered in Narla's gray eyes. "Father—"

He turned on her, stony-faced. "You, too."

"I—?"

"You go to your chambers—and stay there. I wish to be alone with the prisoner."

The girl opened her mouth as if to speak, then closed it again. Flushing slightly under her father's cold, impassive gaze, she stepped through the light-wall into her own quarters.

Now, at last, Zenaor faced the shackled Baemae.

"You know, of course, that you are doomed to die?"

Mutely, the youth nodded.

"Yet there are ways and ways of dying. Slowly, painfully. Quick, clean, easy."

The serf said nothing.

"There are things I would know—things that have to do with Baemae treason." Zenaor's lips drew thin. The black eyes were never colder. "What is this nonsense of someone coming from across the void, from the Federation? You know there are no grounds—that the Federation holds no jurisdiction…"

All the fire seemed to have gone out of the youth. He shrugged sullenly. "All I know is that a one called Tumek learned of some new weapon you planned to use against the free Baemae in the djevoda lands to the south. Secretly, then, he sent word to the Federation, saying that if you ever used such a the thing it would imperil all other worlds as well as ours."

No flicker of emotion showed in Zenaor's lean, high-boned face. "And do you believe him?"

"Who am I to know or judge? Baemae are only good for dying…" The youth gave vent to a bitter laugh. "But at least the far Federation thought the peril was worth a starship."

"And the man—the one they send to weigh the facts here?"

"His name is Craig Nesom. I know no more than that about him."

Silence. An eddying sort of silence that crept in from the walls and up from the floors and down out of the ceiling.

Then, abruptly, the Lord Zenaor laughed.

"So you'll die," he clipped. "But at least you shall go knowing that you're the only man, Baemae or baron, to learn the truth about my weapon. You shall judge it for me with your dying breath—prove to me that it can truly give me power and strength for conquest…"

He was striding away even as he spoke—striding across the room to a wall set off with a delicate interlay of panels.

One slid aside beneath his hand. Beyond lay a chill, bleak laboratory chamber.

Still smiling, Zenaor led the shackled Baemae forward into the laboratory. He then shoved him through a port-like door into a transparent cubicle mounted on a stand.

"Now…one moment." With quick efficiency, the chief of barons closed the cubicle's door and sealed it. Then, taking a tiny glass ampule from the nearest bench, he quickly dropped it into a slot atop the cubicle and brought down a crusher valve upon it.

THE ampule splintered. For an instant light glinted on sparkling, dust-like grains descending, floating out in lazy spirals through the sealed cubicle's still air.

But only for an instant. For then, suddenly, the grains were growing, uniting, multiplying, melding. In a finger-snap, gray slime began to form on the unit's glistening, sterile floor.

A slime that swirled and crawled and eddied…

The shackled serfman screamed.

Not that anyone could hear it. The cubicle was far too skillfully designed for that.

With grim satisfaction, cold appraisal, the Lord Zenaor watched the slime-tide rippling higher. Carefully, he noted reaction time...the victim's grimaces and contortions and frantic terror.

So preoccupied was he that he didn't even hear Narla approaching until her voice rang out behind him, raw with sudden shock, "*Ourobos—!*"

Zenaor spun by instinct.

His daughter's lovely face showed stiff with horror. "Father..." she choked out. Then she retched.

Cold-eyed he waited till the spasm had passed before he spoke, "So...you find my secret shocking?"

"Shocking—?" The girl's eyes held disbelief. "Father, not even Vydys would do such! To bring those horrors here from Xumar—" She shuddered. "You would not! You dare not—"

"I dare not?" Zenaor laughed harshly; gestured to the cubicle and the dying serfman engulfed in slime. "I have already done it."

"Then—you would destroy our world—the Baemae—?" The girl's voice was queer, choked.

"Are there only Baemae, then, on Lysor?" Anger carved Zenaor's jaw-line deeper, sharper. "I am of the Kukzubas, Narla; the barons! My loyalty is to them, for from them I draw my power."

"Your power!" Narla came erect at the word. "There is the answer, father! Your loyalty is not to the barons or to Lysor, but to power alone. You live for it. You bow before no other god."

"And so?" Zenaor stood inflexible as duroid.

The girl gestured helplessly. "What can I say, when not even the fate of our world can touch you?"

"Our world—this puny dot that men call Lysor?" Zenaor laughed aloud. "This planet of ours means nothing, Narla.

By using the slime-things, the ourobos, I can reach out across the void until even the far Federation's chiefs will tremble. Nothing can stop me. *Nothing.*"

"I see." Narla's face was pale now, and her lips quivered. But she stood proud and erect. "Then I have no choice, father. My loyalty is to Lysor. I shall fulfill it."

"Even against me?"

"Even against you."

"So Vydys was right..." The chief of barons' coal-black eyes gleamed hard and bitter. "Very well, then. As of this moment you shall be treated as a prisoner."

The clang of a combox bell cut in upon him. Zenaor left his sentence hanging, flicked the switch. "Yes?"

"My lord, a starship seeks to land here."

"A starship—?" Zenaor stiffened.

"Yes, my lord. The message says it bears an envoy from the Federation."

"His name?"

"Craig Nesom."

Slowly, Zenaor straightened. Cold-eyed, he glanced to the glassite cubicle...the dead serfman, swallowed up in the pulsing slime-mass of the ourobos. He was hardly aware that Narla was stepping quietly from the laboratory chamber.

Again, the voice from the combox, "My lord..."

Harsh-voiced, face set, Zenaor threw back his answer, "Let them land." And then, beneath his breath, "But blasting off alive will be another matter..."

CHAPTER TWO

SHE was the loveliest creature Craig Nesom had ever seen. Or perhaps that was only the hunger gnawing in him— the Earth-hunger, the aching loneliness that comes to all men who dare to roam the far void to the stars.

Yet here he stood, on this strange, mediaevalish world of Lysor.

And here *she* stood before him, smiling.

Suddenly, to Craig Nesom, it didn't matter that they had met in an alien city called Torneulan, or that she was Narla, daughter of Lord Zenaor, whose rule here he had come to question. The crowd's clamor, the bizarre costumes, the twin suns blazing like green balls of fire against an emerald sky, what did they count now? For gazing into this slim girl's eyes, he could almost forget duty and the Federation and the starship, the darkling dreams of friends and homeland.

She said, *"Tarata, jodal...* Welcome, voyager," and he was glad that she paused and smiled and spoke...glad for the psychmen's hypnoscanner treatment that let him understand her words, her meaning.

He matched her pleasantry. "This drink called taxat—will you join me for one?"

"A taxat—?" Her eyes danced. She took his arm. "Of course."

Only then, though her lips still curved, the gray eyes seemed to shadow. Her voice dropped and now, all at once, it held a note of bitterness, of tension, "If death stays its hand long enough for us to drink it."

He stared. *"What—?"*

The shadow vanished. His companion laughed softly; tossed her head in a gesture old as woman, so that the shimmering blonde hair swirled and rippled. Only in her whisper did the dark undercurrent still show through, "Please come. Do not let your face betray us..."

For the fraction of a second Craig hesitated, weighing her with his eyes. He was suddenly acutely aware of alien sounds and smells and voices.

Only then the girl whispered, "Please..." again. Her eyes held mute entreaty.

Stiff, wordless, Craig let her lead him through the throng and din of the assembled barons and their ladies...out of the emerald sunlight, along the shadowy porticos of the tower itself.

The Central Tower. The Tower of Zenaor.

The girl darted a quick glance back over her shoulder, then whispered, "Hurry! We must get out before they realize that we are missing!" Catching Craig's hand in hers, half-running, she pulled him through the nearest door, into the massive building.

There were corridors, then, and stairs and ramps, all leading downward, until at last they moved along a dusty, dim-lit passageway that seemed to stretch forever, echoing and empty.

Abruptly, Craig pulled the girl up short. "It's time for explanations," he stated flatly.

The gray eyes rose to meet his, cool and steady. "You came to Lysor on complaint of Tumek, did you not?"

"Yes."

"And he charged that my father planned aggression that might endanger even your Federation?"

Again, Craig nodded.

119

The girl leaned close. "Do you realize what that means, Craig Nesom? Can you imagine to what lengths the barons will go in order to keep you from reaching Tumek?"

"But—"

A sudden echo of distant voices cut short Craig's answer. The girl went rigid.

"Quick!" Her voice hissed taut, now—ragged. "This may be your only chance to contact Tumek—if it is not too late already!"

After that there was no more time for words, only a hurrying through the silent passage, until at last a ramp loomed before them and they came out into the day once more.

HERE the tower loomed distant and forbidding, a stark shaft lancing up like a spearhead into the emerald sky. Here were the slums, the quarters of the Baemae, with noise and filth and sweat-drenched bodies that stank rank enough to turn the stomach of any Kukzubas baron.

Wordless, still gripping his hand, the girl who was Zenaor's daughter led Craig into a low, cramped wine shop. Dirt scuffed up under his feet. Boisterous voices rang out in shouts and curses, and the stench of stale liquor hung all pervasive. A couple reeled past, clinging to each other for support. The woman's brief halter hung loose. She was laughing drunkenly, and her near-naked body shone slick with sweat. Beyond her, a man prodded a huge, weird, spider-like life form into a shuffling dance atop a table.

Craig's jaw tightened. What was he doing in a place like this? How foolish could even a Federation agent get?

But the girl's gray eyes still pleaded. Tense and raw-nerved, Craig followed her through the crowd and din to a table in the wine shop's farthest corner.

A gaunt, stoop-shouldered oldster paused beside them. He wore the tabard of the serf-class. "Yes?"

"Taxat." The girl spoke for Craig. Her fingers pressed hard against his arm. Her whisper held a note almost of panic, "Quick! Smile, Craig Nesom—before the baron's men suspect the truth and sweep down on us!"

Craig flicked a glance across the room. For the first time he became aware of the presence of solitary loungers—cold-faced, tightlipped men who stood close by the walls, nursing stale drinks.

Their eyes were on him.

The back of his neck prickled. He bared his teeth in a thin, bleak grin. "I might play better if I knew the game," he murmured beneath his breath.

"Oh—?" the girl exclaimed, too loudly. She shot Craig a low-lashed, coquettish glance and pushed closer, sliding her hand over his. Her lips barely moved. "Later, you madman! For now, look at me as men look at woman!"

She drew back as she spoke, flaunting her slim young body's charms before him in a sinuous, sensuous motion. Her face was a pale oval cameo of loveliness. Temptation, incarnate, came to life in the lithe twist of her torso.

Craig caught his breath. "You devil—!"

The red lips quivered. "You see? You learn quickly!" The girl relaxed, leaned against him. "Make love to me, voyager. Your arms—put them about me. Kiss me…"

A numbness gripped Craig. His hands trembled.

But the girl's bare leg and hip pressed hard against him. Her hair brushed his cheek, soft as perfumed silk, and her skin was smoother than any satin. "Are you afraid of me, then, Craig Nesom?"

"Damn you!" he choked.

Only then her cool fingers slid beneath his uniform jacket, and all at once his heart was pounding, pounding. The room, the noise, the cold-eyed loungers—they faded till he could think of nothing but the ripe lips and their invitation.

It was the loneliness, he told himself—the old Earth-hunger.

And here was this woman, Zenaor's own daughter, the antidote, his for the taking.

He would have strained her to him then—in spite of all his doubts and thoughts of Federation rules and duty. But now the serving-serf was back, bearing twin silver cones of taxat.

The girl pushed away from Craig, smoothing her tousled hair. Her face was flushed. Her eyes dodged his.

A sort of senseless fury gripped him. "It's you who are afraid!" he lashed. "You bring me here. You tempt me. But then you push away again—"

The girl's eyes flashed. Once more, she leaned close. Her voice was suddenly edged and brittle. "My task is to help you get to Tumek, Earthman. To that end, and in order to help dispel suspicion, I have no choice but to act like any Kukzubas woman who would rendezvous with a lover in the Baemae quarter. But it goes no further. Now that I have brought you here, a courier will take you on to Tumek. When he comes—"

She broke off sharply, eyes flaring with sudden panic. "Craig—!"

Craig half-turned in his seat.

A MAN stood framed in the wine shop's doorway—a tall broad-shouldered man who wore a high-crowned metal helmet like none that Craig had ever seen before. His sweeping shoulder-cape bore the blaze of brocaded heraldry of Lord Zenaor's service, and his eyes, his mouth, were cruel and grim.

Now he paused on the wine shop's threshold, sweeping the place with a glance that held no mercy.

A hush fell over the echoing, low-ceilinged room—the hush of fear. Men's faces paled, and women shrank back as if to hide behind their partners.

Beside Craig, Narla whispered, "That man—he is my father's chief of guards, the master of the rollers! They must already guess you're on your way to Tumek—"

Once more, Craig glanced round at the doorway—and found himself staring straight into the guard-chief's eyes.

For a taut, vibrant moment the silence echoed. Then the man in the doorway lashed, "On your feet, Earthling..."

Craig felt Narla's nails dig into his arm. Her whisper hissed so faint it might have been imagination, "Window-room behind this..."

A knot drew tight in Craig Nesom's belly. Stiffly, he rose...sidestepped out from behind the table.

The hush of the room was deafening now. The wine shop revelers sat like creatures frozen.

"You die now, Earthling!" snarled the guard-chief. "Here, beneath the rollers, by Lord Zenaor's own orders."

He stepped aside as he spoke. A great, bulbous sphere rolled slowly past him through the doorway.

Instinctively, Craig fell back a step.

"Stop him!" barked the guard-chief.

The words crackled. Two hard-faced loungers by the rear wall sprang forward.

Inside Craig Nesom, something snapped. It came to him suddenly that here lay the answer to all his tension and loneliness and homeland hunger. Here, channeled into rage and bruising violence...

With a curse, he smashed a fist square into the face of the foremost of his assailants. A hoarse cry of anguish burst from the man's throat. He crashed back across the nearest table.

Like lightning, the hand of the second flashed to an ornate belt-dagger.

Craig lunged for him in chill, surging fury. Savagely, he drove his elbow into the soft flesh below the other's rib casing.

The man reeled—retching, knife forgotten.

Craig caught him from behind by belt and shoulder...half-hurled him into the path of the roller that now spun forward.

The Man and sphere came together with a thud of flesh against flesh.

The Man went down, screaming.

But now other guardsmen were charging in. Whirling, Craig dashed for the door to the back room. In another instant he was through it, racing for the window.

A bolt of green fire seared past his head.

He ducked.

But in the same instant, something struck his shoulder a hammer blow from behind. He sprawled on his knees. Through a strange, blurred haze of pain, it dawned on him that now his right arm hung limp and useless.

Only then hands gripped him and dragged him forward, on to the window. Incredulously, he discovered that it was the serving-serf, the gray, stoop-shouldered oldster who had brought the taxat.

"Hurry—!" the man panted. "Climb up! I am not strong enough to lift you..."

With a tremendous effort, Craig dragged himself erect. Clutching the high sill, he tried to pull himself up to it.

The panting serfman heaved and boosted. "Hurry! Hurry—!"

A final surge. Momentarily, Craig sagged on his belly on the sill.

The serf tugged up the banging legs and swung them through the opening.

From behind Craig came a crash of splintering timbers, a ring of curses. He threw a dazed glance back.

Someone—the serf perhaps—had slammed shut a heavy door between this rear room and the wine shop proper.

Now its bolt tore loose. The door burst inward. One of Zenaor's men clawed past it, whipping up a weapon that might have been a pistol.

The old serf threw himself upon the guardsman.

Green fire blazed. The serf fell back.

CRAIG dropped from the window sill into an alley. The haze of pain was clearing now. He could run again, though his right arm still trailed useless at his side.

Desperate, a hunted thing, he plunged off down the passage.

More cries behind him. More green fire blazing.

But these ancient alleys were like a maze, a rabbit warren. Given ten seconds' lead, a man had at least a gambler's chance to lose himself, find safety.

And Craig had ten seconds...ten seconds a gray-thatched serving serf had bought with his own life.

The knowledge brought new sickness surging through Craig—a sickness that drew no fragment from the pain of his wounded shoulder.

But he had no time for thoughts or bitterness or brooding. Not now. For him, there were only the shouts behind and the blackness of the alley.

Only then, from his back trail, a new sound rose...the whisper of a roller's leathery pads spinning over the cobbles.

Craig whirled.

Running blind, caroming from wall to wall as it sped through the narrow alley, the sphere raced towards him.

Craig threw himself into the angle of the nearest doorway.

The sphere missed him by inches and hurtled on beyond.

Sweating, shaking, Craig stepped out once more.

But now the shouts came closer as guardsmen ran towards him, following up the roller.

Pivoting, Craig stumbled on once more.

Before he had taken a dozen steps, the whispering of the roller drifted to him.

The sphere was hurtling back again.

Panting, Craig wedged himself into the chimney-like shaft between two buildings.

Again, the roller passed him. The guards' shouts echoed ever louder.

It dawned on Craig that the crevice in which he stood stretched upward, clear to a tiny wedge of emerald sky.

At least, up there, there'd be no rollers.

Wincing with pain at each movement of his wounded arm, bracing himself with feet on one wall, back against the other, he worked his way slowly up the shaft.

The roller again. Guards below him now.

Craig held his breath.

But they passed on without an upward glance. Painfully, he worked his way still higher, till the emerald wedge widened into a shining vista.

Then—all of a sudden, it seemed—he was out on a flat, sagging roof, drinking in air in great, greedy gulps.

In the same instant, a shout hammered at him. He whirled.

A guard was running towards him across one of the nearby roofs. While he watched, another appeared, then another.

Ring-like, they surrounded him, hemming him in with a circle of death.

And him with no weapon but the rooftop rubble.

Savagely, he cursed aloud—Zenaor, and Lysor, and the Federation, and his job, and duty, and the girl called Narla; baron and Baemae, Earth-worlds and aliens.

Why should he die here, alone and forgotten?

Yet die he would—he knew that now.

But at least, it would cost them.

He fumbled up a brick-sized stone…took his stand against the roof-edge, spraddle-legged.

The guards closed in—warily, now, but moving ever closer.

It was in that moment that the shadow fell across him.

At first Craig thought it was a cloud that had drifted between him and the twin emerald suns.

Then he glimpsed the guards' faces, and knew it was not.

Dropping to one knee, left arm held high to shield his face, he stared up at the thing now skimming towards him.

It was a disc—a shining, circular chip somehow suspended in the sky. A man in a Baemae tabard balanced lithely on it.

Now, while Craig watched, the disc tilted and raced towards him.

A guard shouted. As one, he and his fellows lunged forward.

CRAIG hurled his stone. By more luck than good judgment, it caught the foremost guard square in the forehead.

The man went down like an axed ox. His fellows stopped short.

In the same instant the disc whipped round in a tight spiral close by Craig's side. "Get on! Flat between my legs…" The rider's voice rasped raw and urgent.

Craig threw himself aboard.

Angry cries from the guards. Green fire spurting.

A shout from the discman, "Hold tight!"

Barely in time, Craig caught the disc's rim.

For as he did so, the disc's Baemae rider shifted weight sharply. With startling suddenness, the saucer tilted to a forty-five degree angle.

Another shift. The disc cart wheeled round in a fast spin that had Craig clinging with teeth and toenails.

Then the strange craft was climbing and spinning at once, faster and faster. Even the Baemae pilot dropped to his knees and gripped the disc's edge.

They cleared the roof...peeled off in a wide arc that carried them out and away from the building, still climbing.

The guards' shouts welled to a furious chorus of frustration. Craig glimpsed more streaks of flame.

But they burned out far short of their target. The disc wheeled on, the whole of the ancient Baemae quarter spread out below it.

The serf's fingers dug into Craig's shoulder. He was laughing now—a fierce, bubbling chortle of triumphs. "You see, Earthman? These discs will free Lysor of its thrice-cursed barons! With your aid, Craig Nesom—"

Craig started. "You...know my name—?"

"Did you think I came here to save you by mere chance?" The discman chuckled. "No. I was your contact, to help take you to Tumek. But Zenaor's guardsmen got to you before me. So I stood by and waited, in hopes I could save you."

Craig nodded slowly. "Then you can give me some answers, too—about this whole business."

"A few." The discman straightened. "But that can wait till we have landed..."

Skillfully, he guided the disc off, away from the city; brought it down on a tiny, brush-clotted river island. Stepping clear, he helped Craig up and gripped his hand. "They call me Bukal."

"And you know me already."

They both laughed. Then the discman's broad, bronzed face sobered, "You seek explanations."

"At least, they'd help me," Craig nodded, grinning wryly.

"Then they must be brief. That Zenaor's a devil. He'll trace us in minutes, on a daylight landing." Bukal kicked the disc. "Do you know what this is?"

Craig eyed it curiously. Flat, polished, of plastic or metal, it measured a good six feet across. Beyond that, he could tell little, save that it had neither moving parts nor control equipment, so far as he could see.

"It flies, and it saved my neck," he said finally. "That's all I know about it.

Again, Bukal laughed. A grim laugh without mirth. "Then I'll tell you rover. This thing is a weapon—a weapon of peace, one that can't kill; yet it's going to break the cursed Kukzubas barons' power forever."

"But how—?" Craig groped for words.

"How does it work, you mean?" The bronzed, stocky Bukal chuckled. "Magnetic waves—you know about them?"

"Yes, after a fashion."

"Then think of them flowing from pole to pole like some great river."

Craig stared. "You mean—these discs of yours ride the current—?"

"As chips ride a stream," the other nodded. "The secret lies in the alloy's basic pattern, its molecular structure. It serves as a filter—a trap that catches enough wave-power to lift and carry."

"And to maneuver—"

"You tilt the disc. That breaks the flow-pattern." Shifting, Craig's rescuer peered out through the brush that fringed the river's edge. He gestured. "When our visitors get closer, I'll show you."

CRAIG followed the other's movement; saw a boatload of men in guards' regalia cutting swiftly toward the islet from the river's near shore.

"They're quick," he acknowledged. And then, prompting, he said, "You said discs were weapons."

Bukal's eyes went dark, brooding. "How much do you know of our ways here on Lysor?"

"Only that you have two groups, barons and Baemae—"

"Do you know how the barons hold their power?"

"No."

"They do it with a weapon—a barrier ray, they call it." Bukal's mouth had a bitter twist. "It sets up zones of death around the cities, the great estates—binds us to our serfdom."

"And the discs—"

"They give us a bridge across the barrier—a highway to freedom to end our thousand years of bondage..." Suddenly a tight wolf-grin wiped the bitterness from Bukal's broad face. He surged to his feet. "Here. Let me show you!"

A cry of excitement rose from the guardsmen out on the river. The boat arced towards Craig and bronzed Bukal.

The Baemae laughed aloud. Bending, he seized the disc and lifted it on edge. "You see? It is light."

Craig brought up his own hand beneath it. For all its size, the thing seemed hardly heavier than balsa.

Gesturing him back, Bukal swung the disc clear of the ground, holding it waist-high, plate-flat. "Now, I spin it..." He whipped it round as if its center were mounted on a pivot, pulling through with his right hand, guiding with the left.

The boat was almost to the island now. The guards were readying their weapons.

Faster, till the wave-flow catches. The disc was spinning like a top now, parallel with the ground.

Craig threw a quick glance at the guard boat. A trickle of sweat rolled down his spine.

He looked back to Bukal and the saucer.

Suddenly, there was the slightest of jerks. The disc seemed to vibrate.

Bukal dropped his hands. For a moment the disc hung in the air, spinning free.

And then, incredibly, instead of falling, slowly it began to rise!

Open-mouthed, Craig stared, still not quite believing.

But already Bukal was moving. Nimbly, he threw himself forward, flat on the disc.

The plate stopped spinning. As if by magic, it hung suspended in the air, swaying gently.

Bukal clambered to his feet, balancing on the polished surface as a bather might upon a surfboard. Tilting skillfully, he sideslipped the strange craft down a fraction lower. "Get on!"

Sucking in a breath, Craig slid aboard.

Bare yards away, the boat beached. Guards swarmed ashore, cursing and shouting.

Nonchalantly, Bukal threw them a salute, and brought the disc round in a lazy, climbing spiral.

Green fire, falling short. Fuming rage, wild curses.

"You see—?" The elation of triumph rang in Bukal's voice. "It's the end of the barons, Earthman! How can any barriers hold back the Baemae, when with discs like this we can sail above them? To the south, there's the whole djevoda range and freedom! Already, we've colonies of our own down there, free colonies, spread out so the barons can't strike at them. We're turning out these discs by hundreds—emptying the cities, stripping the estates to their last serfman—"

Frowning, narrow-eyed, Craig stared down at the panorama spread out below them, then off to the glittering towers of Torneulan.

"Why send for me, then?" he cut in on the other. "Who's Tumek? What made him call for help from the Federation?"

The discman's face sobered. "Why—?" He shrugged. "That I can't tell you; it's still Tumek's secret."

"And…who is he?"

"Tumek?" Light came back to Bukal's bronzed face. "Call him genius; that says it."

"But—"

"A statue-caster by trade; old, now; one of the free Baemae craftsmen. These discs—he devised them. The colonies, too—they're part of his plan."

"Yet he sent for help…" Craig's frown deepened.

"He heard rumors of some new scheme of Zenaor's." Bukal shifted, glanced up into the darkening sky. Tilting the disc, he crept it in towards the outskirts of the city's bleak Baemae quarter. "When the green day suns, Boh and Koh, set, and night comes, I'll drop you off near him. He's hiding in the shop of a friend, Notal, in the Street of Arts, waiting for you."

Craig nodded slowly. Thoughtfully, he looked away to the west, where the nose of the starship showed above the buildings like a slim silver lance-tip. "Good. Meantime…"

"Yes?"

"Meantime—"

IT was a sentence never finished.

Suddenly, out of a gap in the roof of a ruined building below them, a blurred bulky mass vomited towards them. Spreading as it hurtled upward, it stretched into loose-patterned cordage.

Bukal went rigid. "A net-gun—!" He sideslipped the disc. It careened low over the hovels.

But green flame speared up in their path—a great, roaring gout of it, ten times the size of the blast that might come from any hand weapon.

Bukal jerked back. The disc spun crazily.

Then they were falling, men and disc alike, clinging precariously. Barely in time, the craft leveled off a fraction, then tilted once more to spill both Craig and Bukal to the ground, a jarring, ten-foot fall.

Guardsmen lunged up from cover, converging upon them.

Craig lurched to his feet, trying to shake the haze from his eyes.

But Bukal was ahead of him—shoving him bodily back into an alley. "Run for it, you fool! I'll hold them—"

Staggering, half-falling, Craig fled into the shadows.

The starship. That was the answer. If he could only reach the starship! This thing was beyond any one man's handling...

Panting, he crawled up a crumbling stair, searching the skyline for some glimpse of the silver prow to guide him.

Then there it was, off to the west.

Craig's jaw tightened. That slim silver craft represented the strength of the whole Federation. One word from it and a fleet would come roaring down upon Lysor.

But first, that word must be spoken.

He phrased the message in his mind: "DETAILS LACKING BUT NO DOUBT OF ZENAOR AGGRESSIVE INTENTIONS AS SHOWN IN ATTEMPTS TO KILL ENVOY..."

He started to turn, to make his way back down the stairs.

But in that instant the sky went suddenly bright with a blaze of light—a light so dazzling that it left Craig blind and shaking.

A light that centered on the starship.

Craig clapped his hands across his eyes. A wave of sudden panic gripped him.

Grimly—desperately, almost—he fought it down.

Slowly, his vision cleared. He let his hands fall.

Then he wished he had not.

For now the starship's silver prow no longer stood silhouetted against the distant western sky. As if by magic, it had vanished, its passage marked only by a slowly settling dust-smoke haze.

So this was Zenaor's answer to the Baemae challenge. He had destroyed the Federation starship.

Craig Nesom stood on Lysor alone…

CHAPTER THREE

THE Street of Arts—narrow and winding, lined with the small, cramped shops of skilled craftsmen who wrought wondrous things of wood and leather, glass and metal. Here you could buy the finest filigree of silver...paintings on porcelain or plastic figurines carved from djevoda tusks...fabrics that glinted with threads of Xumarian thrill and Odak's orslan.

And here hid Tumek.

Tumek, the statue-caster. Tumek, the sculptor.

Tumek, genius of the Baemae...the man who had devised the flying disc and harnessed the power that surged through his world's magnetic waves.

Yet even Tumek had cringed before Zenaor's sadistic schemings and pleaded across a million drals of void for Federation aid.

Now, on Bukal's word, he lay in hiding here in the shop of his fellow caster Notal, waiting for the Federation's envoy to arrive.

At least, Craig Nesom hoped so.

Pausing in the shadows across from Notal's shop, he hesitated for a moment, studying the darkened front with its display of busts that peered out, wan and ghostlike, in the blue night-sun Roh's dim light.

Somewhere at the back of the shop, a gleam of yellow flickered.

So there was really someone there. Taut-nerved, Craig started forward.

Only then, off to his right, metal clanged on metal.

Craig froze again.

More sounds crept to him…sounds of shuffling feet, of men in movement.

Silent as any specter, he drew back against the building behind him…slid left along it till he was lost in the pitch-black angle where the next shop joined it.

The shuffling feet drew nearer. Craig caught the hiss of whispering voices. Shapes took form—the shapes of men stalking stealthily, skulking in the shadows.

Warily, Craig edged forward a fraction and peered along the front of the shop to his left.

But here, too, shapes were emerging from the murk. A stray blue beam glinted on what might have been a weapon.

Craig slid back into his angle.

The two groups met in mid-street, scant yards out from him. There was a buzz of whispered consultation. Then, silently, both groups drew back. The men spread out, ranging themselves along the wall on his side of the street.

Craig held his breath.

But already one figure was shuffling towards him, slouching against the wall bare inches from his shoulder. "A curse on the Baemae and their plots!" the intruder muttered. "Night's a time for wine and wenches, not for raiding."

Craig grunted wordless affirmation.

The stranger turned; peered at him. "Who are you, friend? Which company?" And then, in sudden shock: "You! You're not—"

With all his might, Craig slashed a stiff hand-edge across the other's windpipe, his Adam's apple. The man's voice cut off in mid-syllable.

Craig crashed the heel of his hand up under a stubbled chin, thanking the stars that his shoulder was no longer stiff.

The intruder's head snapped back against the stonework. Hard.

Then his knees were buckling. He started to fall.

Craig caught him, held him erect.

In the same instant a whistle shrilled. The other shadow-skulkers leaped forward from their hiding places, converging on the shop across the street where Tumek had his refuge. They made no effort at concealment now. There were shouts; a splintering crash as the door burst in.

ICY sweat drenched Craig. Shaking, he eased his unconscious prisoner to the ground in the shadows of the angle and stripped him of the weapon in his belt—one of the pistol-things that blazed green fire.

Inside Notal's shop, another door went down. Craig glimpsed struggling figures silhouetted against a backdrop of yellow light.

All along the street, windows swung wide and doors opened. Lights flared. Voices rang out in a startled babble.

A man appeared in the entrance of the shop before which Craig stood, rubbing sleep from his eyes. "What—?"

In three quick steps Craig was beside him—jamming the fire-gun against his fat belly; shoving him back on his own tracks into the building; slamming and bolting the door behind them.

Fear flared in the fat man's button eyes. His blubbery face went slack.

"Quiet!" Craig stabbed the pistol against him harder. "One sound and I kill you!"

The other's mouth worked, but no words came. He tottered backward and slumped down onto a bench.

Craig opened the door a crack and shot a quick glance out.

The raiders were leaving Notal's shop now. They dragged a captive with them, a short, balding man whose face showed the wrinkles of age.

Craig turned back to his own prisoner. "Who is that?"

The fat man's voice shook, "He is called Tumek."

Tumek…

A chill shook Craig Nesom. Across the street, the last of the raiders inside the shop paused by the display window. Deliberately, he picked up one bust after another and smashed it. The last he hurled through the window itself, then swaggered out to join the others. Their laughter echoed raucously.

Then someone barked a command. The laughter ceased. With chill efficiency a group fell in, formed a double rank facing Notal's shop.

Another command. Two of the guardsmen caught the prisoner by the arms and jerked him forward, slamming him back hard against one of the uprights of the shop-front. Then, quickly, they stepped aside.

Again, the harsh voice of command.

The double rank raised weapons.

Inside the shop across the street, Craig went rigid.

Out there, mere feet away, stood the man who'd brought him to this planet, the Baemae genius, Tumek.

Tumek, the one man who could tell him the things he so needed to know—the baron's plans; the dreams and schemes and power of Zenaor.

Only Tumek stood before a firing squad. Ten seconds more and he'd be dead.

Craig acted by instinct then, not logic.

Quite coolly, he brought up the fire-gun he'd taken from the guardsman…leveled it with grim precision at the squad's commander.

The man passed some remark to Tumek, but the oldster only shook his head and stood the straighter, face calm, serene almost spiritual.

Craig corrected his aim a fraction.

The firing squad's commander pivoted...sucked in air to give the final order.

Craig squeezed the fire-gun's trigger.

A green shaft of flame lanced out. It struck the squad chief square in the chest. He slammed backward—face contorted in a death's-head grimace; already toppling.

The squad seemed to freeze in its tracks. Then, as the spell broke, one man started to whirl, whipping round his own weapon.

Craig dropped him where he stood.

Chaos descended on the guardsmen. Frantically, they lunged for cover.

CROUCHED, shadow-silent, Craig slipped from the shop and moved through the murk towards the spot where the prisoner had stood, trusting to confusion and the dark to shield him. "Tumek..."

Someone roared, "Look out! It's the Earthman!"

The night turned dazzling green with fire-blasts.

Craig dived through the shop's shattered window, skidding across the floor on one shoulder.

A hand clutched his arm. A cracked voice choked, "Craig Nesom—!"

Craig twisted. Tumek's wrinkled face loomed, a dim blur in the gloom.

"Quick! This way—" The old man wormed towards the rear of the building.

Craig followed.

Only then a dark figure was rising and shouting. A fire-gun blazed, close at hand.

Craig shot back. The looming antagonist fell away.

Old Tumek fell with him.

Stumbling to his feet, Craig heaved up the oldster's limp body. With a strength born of sheer desperation, heedless of shouts and fire-blasts, he lunged on, out the rear door of the building.

A guard rose in their path.

Craig shot him down and charged blindly on, deep into the black alley shadows.

A thin whisper from Tumek, "Right... next crosspath...Door unlocked..."

Craig veered. In seconds he was pushing past a heavy gate...easing it shut behind him once more.

The sounds of the guards' rage faded. Gently, Craig lowered Tumek to the ground.

An acrid scent rose in his nostrils—the scent of charred flesh. With a shock, he became aware of the old Baemae's hoarse, labored breathing.

Numbly, he ran cautious fingers over the other's withered body.

The flesh along Tumek's right rib-casing *crackled!*

Then, slowly, the old eyes opened. The cracked voice spoke, the faintest of whispers, "You...are the Earthman— the Federation agent?"

Mute, sick, Craig nodded.

"Good." The eyes closed again, as if suddenly too heavy.

But only for a moment: "Earthman..."

"Yes."

"Ourobos...from Xumar—they are Zenaor's weapon."

"Ourobos—?" Craig strained close. "Tumek, what are they?"

"A...life-form. Zenaor's daughter can tell you." The voice of the old Baemae grew weaker.

"Zenaor's daughter—!"

"Yes. Narla…"

"But—"

"Only…one weapon… against ourobos—crystal."

"Crystal—?"

"Ourobos…" The old man's face was slack now, his words thick and mumbled. It was as if he could no longer hear Craig's questions. "Other planets, too…not just Lysor. That's…why I asked help. Zenaor…dreams of conquest."

"Tumek…" Craig choked. "Tumek, the crystal—tell me about that!"

But again, he could not know if the other even heard.

"Narla…"the old man whispered, "see Narla…" And then he muttered, "Disc…on roof…here…"

THE words died in a rattle. Muscles tensed in a small convulsive movement. The mouth fell open. The old head sagged back.

Tumek died.

For a long, long moment, Craig Nesom slumped beside him.

It was no end for genius. Not here, in a dirt-floored hovel off an alley.

Only that was death's way. It paid no heed to propriety or convenience.

Nor to right, either, nor the needs of men.

Without Tumek, the Baemae cause might go down to disaster. Lord Zenaor could yet live to fulfill his dream of conquest, carve his path across the universe with the ourobos.

Unless the crystal stopped him.

"The crystal"—that was all Tumek had said about it. Not what it was, nor how to use it.

But…there was still Narla.

Narla, of the cool gray eyes and flaxen hair. Narla, who laughed and tempted—and then went cold with sudden fury.

Narla, Lord Zenaor's own daughter.

Tumek had said to see her.

Slowly, Craig got up. Stiff, shuffling, weary, he made his way to the room's one slot-like window.

The night outside was brighter now, blue with Roh's chill rays. The Kukzubas towers loomed sleek and shining, sheer to the very sky.

And there was the Central Tower. Also the Tower of Zenaor—rising even higher and more starkly than the rest.

How could any man hope to get into that grim crypt to talk to Narla? Every door would be locked, every entrance guarded.

At least, on the lower levels.

But higher, perhaps…

Thoughtfully, Craig appraised the towering structure.

Invading it would be madness, pure and simple.

And yet, with the starship shattered, what did he have to lose?

Besides, Zenaor owed him a debt…a debt that only blood could cancel.

Blood. The blood of the starship's crew, and of the Baemae. Of Tumek, and a gray-thatched serving-serf without a name.

And on the roof here, Tumek had said, a disc lay ready.

A disc, and a debt of blood, and the Tower of Zenaor.

And Narla.

Why was he hesitating?

Cold-eyed, tight-lipped, Craig Nesom groped towards the stair…

CHAPTER FOUR

THE disc came down to the roof like a drifting feather. Stepping from it, Craig paused for a moment, staring out with brow furrowed at the spangled night of Torneulan. City of barons or city of Baemae, there was beauty here in this silent moment.

Only now was no time for beauty. Not here, atop Lord Zenaor's sleek, shining fortress tower.

Craig turned.

A stair-housing rose near one edge of the flat, parapeted roof. Crossing to it, he kicked out the door's translucent panel.

Inside, now. The stairwell yawned like a black, bottomless pit. Silently, Craig crept down the steps.

There was another locked door at the bottom—and this one had no panel.

Craig kicked it.

It held firm. He kicked it again—unrestrained, now—and again, and again, till the echoes rang round him in thunder chorus.

From beyond the portal came a beat of running feet. Someone fumbled with the door's handle.

Craig drew his fire-gun…waited.

The door opened, a bare inch.

Craig kicked it with all his might.

The door burst open. A guard reeled back, clutching his face where the swinging edge had struck him.

Craig kicked him, too—first in the belly; then, when he doubled over, in the face.

The guard crumpled and lay still.

Craig strode down the hall, trying doors. But the rooms they sealed were empty, unfinished.

Craig went back to the guard.

The man was moaning now. His fingers dug spasmodically at the naked tiles of the floor.

Dragging him erect, Craig shoved him back flat against the wall.

Slowly, the other's sagging head lifted. The glazed eyes cleared a little.

Craig held his voice cold and level, "Where's Zenaor?"

"At…this hour?" The swollen lips bubbled. "Down—seventh level."

"And between?"

"The guest chambers—Lady Vydys—her party."

"Vydys…" Craig paused—frowning, searching his memory. Where had he heard that name before? From Tumek, or Narla? Or in a report, while he briefed for this mission?

He scowled, probing. "Why are you here, then, when this level's empty?"

"Why—? With Vydys in the tower?" The bloodshot eyes widened. "My lord Zenaor loves life. He knows better than to trust her."

The memories came back with a rush, if not their source. Vydys the Cruel, chief of all Zenaor's rivals! Here, in this tower, tonight!

Craig drew his lips thin.

"Where's your post, scum?"

"Below—force shaft." The guard gestured. "Heard you—kicking."

Craig stepped aside. "Get back to it, then." He motioned with the fire-gun.

The guard shot him a bleared, uncertain glance. Then, shuffling, not quite steady, one hand to the wall, the man moved ahead of Craig down the hall to an alcove backed with twin sliding panels. Clutching the grip of the one of the right, he pushed it back.

Beyond lay a small, square room like a closet, but without floor or ceiling.

The guard stepped across the threshold. It was as if he had moved out onto an invisible platform. Erect, motionless, he sank slowly down the shaft.

Craig shot one breath-taking glance into the pit, and followed.

INSTANTLY, a pulsing vibrance seemed to grip and hold him. Taut-nerved, he stood rigid, drifting slowly down against the lift of an upward flow of some strange current.

Below him, the guard reached out and caught a metal handhold jutting from the shaft's wall, then slid back a panel like the one above and stepped out into broad hall.

But where the top level had shown stark and bare, here lay luxury to stagger man's imagination. The walls were a shimmering tapestry of translucent color. Craig's feet sank into raaltex carpeting so thick and soft that it was like stepping onto a cloud.

He gripped the guard's arm. "Now—Vydys!"

"This way." The other turned, shuffling ahead. "End chamber…"

Craig shifted the fire-gun in his hand; laid the butt hard across the guard's head behind the ear.

The other crumpled to the floor, unconscious. Stripping off the man's harness, Craig donned the livery himself and lashed his prisoner's wrists and ankles, rolling him out of sight behind a long, sofa-like seat.

Then he was at the door, the door to the Lady Vydys' chambers.

He paused for a moment, listening with his ear against the panel.

No sound came.

He gripped the handle…turned it slowly…let the weight of his shoulder press against the door.

Ever so slowly, it swung open a fraction. Craig peered into the living room beyond—a place fully as ornate as the corridor, with furnishings sleekly trimmed in polished chromite.

Craig slipped inside and closed the door behind him.

On the far side of the room, another door stood open. Noiselessly, Craig crossed to it…looked into a bedroom. A sleeping-couch, all gold and white, rested against the far wall, framed in darkly glinting mirrors.

While he watched, the coverlet moved. A body shifted.

Gripping the fire-gun, Craig walked warily to the couch-side.

Black hair rippled against white pillows. A sleek body twisted—sensuous, cat-like.

Then the head turned. For the first time, Craig saw the face.

A woman's face. The face of evil, incarnate, living in the fleshly form that men called Lady Vydys.

Yet she was lovely. Even here, even now, Craig Nesom's heart pounded as he looked down on her.

He rested his weight against a chair arm; raised the fire-gun. "Vydys…"

She stirred in her sleep. The shadow of a frown crossed the lovely face.

"Vydys!"

Slowly, the soot-black lashes lifted. The dark eyes opened.

Craig said softly, "Quiet my lady! Don't make me kill you!"

She showed no sign of fear—no sudden tensing, no quick tremor.

"You know, of course, that your heart will be torn from your body for this, carrion." Her voice was low and silky.

"Will it?" Mirthlessly, Craig chuckled.

Vydys' black eyes widened. She twisted beneath the coverlet. "You are no guardsman..." And then—staring, rocked back with sudden shock and said, "You—the Earthman..."

"Yes, the Earthman," Craig nodded bleakly.

"But—what do you want—?"

"You know a girl called Narla? Zenaor's daughter?"

The dark eyes narrowed. "Yes..."

"Would you trade me even for her?"

A note of bafflement; a shifting.

"Trade you...even...?"

"Yes." Craig leaned forward. "I want her, Vydys—and I'll give you Zenaor's own head for her..."

Vydys' hand came up to the ripe swell of her bosom. Scarlet lips peeled back from small, sharp white teeth. "Zenaor's head?"

Again, Craig nodded. He let his own lips part in a tight wolf-grin. "Let's talk straight, Vydys. You hate Zenaor for his power as chief of barons. You know that the first safe chance he gets he'll cut your lovely throat."

"And so—?"

"So your only chance is to get him first—before he finishes the Baemae and decides to turn his full force on you."

An irregularity developed in Vydys' breathing. The dark eyes smoldered. "You…would help me with this, Earthman?"

Wordless, Craig tilted his head in affirmation.

"Now…tonight…?"

"Yes."

"But why? What is your reason?"

Craig smiled—a crooked smile. "I said I wanted Zenaor's daughter Narla, Vydys. That means alive—both of us. I'll need help to handle it."

THE last traces of Vydys' hesitation vanished. She twisted; sat up on the sleeping-couch, her face aglow with dark excitement.

"He is on the seventh level, Earthman. If anyone should question, tell him that you carry a message to Zenaor for me. Here, take this signet—" She stripped a ring set with a carved black gem from a slender finger and held it out to Craig.

Not touching it, he said, "I've got a better idea."

Vydys' smooth brow furrowed ever so slightly. "What—?"

"You go with me."

She caught her breath.

"You see?" Craig laughed harshly. "The picture changes when your neck's in the noose along with mine." He got up and gestured peremptorily with the fire-gun. "Come on…"

Her nostrils flared. "And if I will not?"

Craig paused; brought his weapon's muzzle up, steady and level. "A blast from this at close range would sear your breasts till they crackled, my lady."

A quick-drawn breath. Fear was in the dark eyes now—fear, and…something else, something strange, hard to define.

Then, wordless, the woman slid from the bed and pulled on shoes and a diaphanous outer garment.

Craig came close behind her and said, "Time's short."

She shrugged; leaned against him for a moment. "Why do you want her, Earthman—that pale slut, Narla?"

Involuntarily, Craig stiffened, then stood wooden-faced, unmoving. "Why does any man want a woman, my lady?"

"A woman—?" Vydys' laugh held an edge of scorn…or was it fury? "You call that creature a woman, Earthman? There's water in her veins, not blood!"

Craig stepped away from her, not answering.

For an instant lines of quick anger slashed Vydys' face. Then the tempest faded. Together, the two of them, they went out through the corridor to the force shaft. They rode it down in pulsing silence to the seventh level. Walked echoing halls where the tension crawled like a living thing.

Ahead, an intersection loomed. Down the right-hand passage, a guard paced slowly.

Vydys breathed, in sharply. "There—he watches over Zenaor's chambers…"

Craig pushed her forward.

The guard came about, his face a bleak mirror of suspicion. His hand hovered by his weapon.

Vydys said, "I seek the Lord Zenaor."

"At this hour?" Irritation pushed aside distrust. "My lord sleeps."

Ever so casually, Craig eased closer.

"Are you sure?" Vydys' hand came up in a helpless, perplexed gesture. "They told me—"

Craig turned and sidestepped, as if to hear them both the better.

The guard scowled. "Listen—"

Craig brought up a hand as if to scratch his head—and then, pivoting, smashed a blow to the guard's temple.

The man staggered, clawing for his weapon.

Craig caught his wrist in both hands; twisted.

It spun the other around—off balance, still staggering. A kick to the back of his knees buckled his legs. He sprawled flat on his face.

Then, before Craig could move, Vydys threw herself on their fallen foeman like a tigress. A slender, stiletto-like knife flashed in her hand, lancing down into the soft hollow at the base of the guard's skull.

The man's body jerked once, spasmodically, then lay still.

VYDYS came to her feet in one smooth, sinuous motion. She was breathing hard. A strange, hot light of excitement gleamed in her eyes.

Craig snatched the bloody knife out of her hand. "Why did you do that? We could have tied him—"

"So that he could talk later?" Teeth bared, she laughed, high and keening. "No, Earthman! This way is better!"

Craig looked from the dead guard to the knife. He could feel the hair along the back of his neck rising.

As if reading his thoughts, Vydys laughed again, low this time—taunting. "Did you think to find me defenseless, Earthman? Me, Vydys of Cadilek?" She swayed close against him. "You have daring, warrior! That is why I came with you—not out of fear."

Craig pushed past her. "Come on, then—before Zenaor's men surprise us." Bending, he dragged the dead guard up by the harness.

Vydys' face was a mask, the dark eyes unfathomable. She turned and pulled back the door's handle.

The portal swung open. Wordless, Craig followed her into the room beyond, dragging the corpse with him.

A man's quarters, these—bleak, severe, without ostentation. Here no mirror walls threw back the glint of polished chromoid. The raaltex carpeting of the chambers above in this room was replaced with ostran tile and schalagat.   Dark leathers gleamed dully against the flat contrast of iron-gray duroid.

Cat-like, slim Vydys tiptoed to the sleeping chamber's entry. Her breath hissed in the stillness as she looked in.

Taut-nerved, Craig lowered the dead guard to the floor.

But already Vydys was back beside him, slim hand out-thrust. "My knife—" It was a command.

Craig stepped past her, not answering. In his turn, he peered through the arch into the other chamber.

Zenaor lay there, sleeping. Yet even at rest, the lean, high-boned face showed no trace of slackness. The muscled hands still curled to fists.

"My knife…" Vydys whispered again, close to Craig's ear. "You promised me his head, Earthman."

Craig stared down at her.

The dark eyes glowed like twin coals now, and the skin of her face seemed suddenly to have stretched tighter, replacing curves with planes and hollows. The fingers that strained towards the dagger trembled with a naked urgency, somehow obscene, as if in the bloodlust of this moment the woman's very soul were spread out to the viewer, dark and evil.

Craig turned away…looked again at the sleeping Zenaor.

"Curse you, Earthman—!" Vydys panted. She clawed for the knife.

For an instant their bodies strained together in silent struggle. Then, suddenly, Vydys ceased to writhe and twist. Her body pulsed against Craig's.

His heart pounded. He clutched the woman to him.

A voice said, "If you move, you die!"

Craig froze. Ever so slowly, he brought his head round.

Narla stood framed against a drape-shrouded door to his right. She gripped a fire-gun in her hand.

She raised her voice before he could speak. "Father!"

Zenaor came awake with a twist, a jerk of covers. The coal-black eyes gleamed beneath the heavy brows. "So— visitors!" And then, to Narla: "My daughter…"

"It's nothing. They spoke too loudly. I heard them."

The fire-gun in her hand stayed very steady.

"You'll not regret it." Zenaor groped a weapon of his own from a stand by his sleeping-couch. His lips set in a thin, mirthless smile. "Welcome, Vydys. You come in strange company."

"He…forced me…"

"He forced you!" Mockery rang in Zenaor's harsh laughter. And then, the mirth dying: "Woman, you go back to your chambers. Under open guard, this time, with every man ordered to kill you if you so much as smile at him."

Vydys' lovely face flushed. "Zenaor, you dare not!"

"Because if I do you'll kill me?" Zenaor's voice suddenly echoed flat menace. "You'll try, you mean, you wench—just as you tried here, tonight. And you'll fail again. Only perhaps by then I'll have less need to let you live for the sake of Kukzubas unity, and I can watch you writhe and die instead, as you should die now!"

There was silence, then—a taut, hate—surging silence. Eyes smoldering, white to the lips, Vydys smoothed her gown, her hair.

ZENAOR turned to Craig Nesom, "You, Earthman— now you, too, shall join ranks with your fellows who died in the starship."

Craig shrugged. In this tumor, this place, words were wasted.

"But slowly," the chief of barons continued. "There are many things I would ask you—things best brought out under torture: how you got here into my chambers; the plans of the

Baemae; your relations with Vydys. So, you die—but by inches."

Craig shrugged again.

The baron's eyes narrowed. A spark that might have been grim mirth lighted behind them. "And...there is another thing you should know..." He spoke almost softly. "Your serf genius, Tumek, sought to defeat me. With this."

Left-handed, he reached into the stand beside the sleeping-couch once more, and brought out a flat, black case perhaps six inches across. His thumb touched a spring. The cover flew open.

A great crystal gleamed on black Orlon.

In spite of himself, Craig Nesom went rigid.

"You see? It ends here!" Zenaor chuckled. "What it means, how the serfs were to use it against the weapon I plan to defeat them with, I do not know. But whatever its purpose, I have it, and its maker lies dead."

He snapped shut the case, dropped it back into the stand. "Back, now, both of you, while I call the guards."

The pulse in Craig Nesom's temple pounded. Turning, he started past Narla towards the door.

Her gray eyes dodged his. She stepped aside, fire-gun lowered.

"Guards..." That was Zenaor, at the com-box.

Craig stopped breathing, stopped thinking. Like lightning striking, he leaped sidewise, pivoting back, behind Narla.

Zenaor roared a curse.

But already, Craig was clawing the girl close against him, snatching her fire-gun, blazing a flare straight at the baron.

Zenaor dived over the sleeping-couch. The fireball seared into the wall.

Craig jammed the gun against Narla. "Zenaor! If I die, she burns with me!"

Time stood still. Silence echoed.

Again Craig lashed out, "Do you love her, Zenaor? Do you want her to burn?"

He could hear the rasp of the other's quick-drawn breath. "Curse you, Earthman—!"

"And curse *you*, Zenaor!" New recklessness surged through Craig. "Curse you for all the blood you've shed; your arrogance, your lust for power, your cruelty—" And then: "Vydys! Bring me that crystal!"

Tension. The fire-gun's muzzle leveled.

Wordless, the woman obeyed.

Craig gripped the jewel case. "I'm leaving now, Zenaor— and Narla goes with me. Warn your guards of that."

Silence again, broken only by the sound of heavy breathing.

Craig drew Narla back, tight against him, a living shield. Holding her close, he backed through the exit door. The girl was trembling now. He could feel her heart pound.

Then they were out in the corridor once more...the same bleak, echoing passageway through which he'd come with dark Vydys.

Only that seemed an eternity ago, now.

Jerking the door shut, dragging the girl by one wrist, Craig raced for the force shaft. Slamming back the panel on the downside, he jammed it ajar. Then, sliding open the other unit, he pulled Narla into the lift-current, closed the gate behind them, and let go of the hand-hold.

Together, they surged upward, level after level.

Narla's face showed pale and drawn. "Where...are you taking me?"

Craig laughed aloud. His head swam, as if he were suddenly drunk on danger and recklessness and tension. "You'll see."

Overhead, the shaft-cap loomed closer...closer. They reached the top level, hung there, suspended.

Then Craig slid back the panel, and they stepped out into the bare, echoing hallway's darkness. Still gripping the girl's wrist, he groped his way up the stairway and out onto the flat top of the tower.

THE disc still lay where he had left it. Far to the west, the sky was already turning turquoise, Roh's blue beams dimming. In minutes the great green morning sun called Bah would climb above the far horizon.

Pulling Narla to the edge of the roof, Craig peered down.

Ant-like, men were moving through the street below—spreading out, forming a cordon.

"Too bad I'll have to miss the reception." He chuckled and turned bad to Narla. "Now; about the crystal—"

"The crystal—?" Her gray eyes clouded. "I know nothing of it."

Craig stared. "But Tumek said—"

"He sent it to me to hold for him. That was all. He never told me its use."

A numbness gripped Craig.

The girl said, "Besides, even if I did know, why should I trust you—you, who came as murderers come, with that creature Vydys to whom only pain is passion?"

Craig turned on her. "What—?"

"You held her, did you not? Else how could I surprise you—?"

"Are you jealous, then—because it was she I held, and not you?"

Narla's face turned white with fury. "Not even a sadat would say such a thing!" She jerked free of Craig's hand, beat her small fists on his chest. "Go, you rabble! Leave me! Go back to the scum, the Baemae!"

Craig reached for her hands.

She jumped back and slapped his face.

The sting of her palm was like a trigger. With a curse, he lunged for her and caught her to him, still struggling and flailing.

"Is this what you want?" Savagely, brutally, he kissed her.

Her lips were like ice. Her eyes blazed gray fire. "Is that quite all, Earthman?"

Craig sucked in air. "No. Not quite." Pinioning her arms, once again he glanced down at the cordon of guards in the street below. "You see...you're going with me."

"No!"

"Yes." He flashed a tight, hard grin. "Without a knowledge of how to use Tumek's crystal, the Baemae will need a weapon against your father. And what better could they find than you, his daughter, as a hostage?"

Shoving her aside, he lifted the great disc from the rooftop; spun it.

It jerked...caught...hovered.

"Please, Craig Nesom..."

"Please indeed, my lady Narla! We're sailing south this morning—away from Torneulan, beyond the reach of your father and his cursed Kukzubas barons."

"You mean—?"

"Yes." Bodily, he lifted her and set her on the hovering disc. "We are traveling south to the djevoda range, and freedom..."

CHAPTER FIVE

BELOW them now stretched rolling grasslands, mile after green-gold mile. Afar, the darker green of shrubs and trees marked waterholes or fringed the meandering streams that glinted in the clear white light of Yoh, Lysor's midday sun. A fragrance of flowers, of foliage—drifted upward even to the disc, high above it all, still gliding southward.

A paradise, it was. But a paradise apparently without human population. Craig still could find no sign of habitation—only the tiny, moving dots that were herds of some unknown animal grazing.

Then, off to the west, a thin wisp of smoke curled skyward.

Craig shifted his weight so that the disc wheeled towards the distant streamer. "Narla..."

The girl's blonde head moved just a fraction—barely enough to tell him that she, too, saw the far-off feather. That was all. She didn't speak.

A little of Craig's elation left him. Again, as a thousand times before, he wondered about the slim girl crouching on the disc between his feet.

She was Zenaor's daughter.

Yet...she had also helped to bring him, Craig Nesom, into contact with the Baemae.

Whose side was she really on?

Or did she even know herself?

Craig wondered.

But whatever the answer, she was here with him, in his power, his weapon to break her father's grip on Lysor.

He should have been glad for it. It was what he'd sought, the thing he needed to help avenge his friends who'd died aboard the starship. Only somehow, now, it brought no sense of surging triumph. If anything, the thing he felt was guilt, an ugly gnawing of his own conscience because he'd forced her to come with him.

Ahead, a huddle of buildings came into view below the smoke-wisp.

Craig changed course a fraction.

The buildings showed clearer now—shanties straggling out behind a palisade, across a broad, hill-sheltered plain that sloped down gently to a river. For the first time, Craig could see people moving about.

He tilted the disc, coasting down towards the village in a long, looping arc.

But now those below glimpsed the saucers. A flurry of excitement flared. Fingers pointed. Men ran towards the largest of the buildings.

But not for shelter. For suddenly they were back again, out in the open, carrying discs. In seconds a whole company had taken to the air.

Craig banked sharply as they raced towards him.

But a fierce cry rang out from above him. He jerked around just in time to see a host of other discs slashing down out of the blue.

Then one peeled off, lanced closer. Craig glimpsed a lean, half-naked body...bared teeth...a fierce bronzed face.

The rider's arm snaked out. A long black whip flicked towards Craig. Before he could move, the lash twined about his up-flung wrist.

The rider above twisted sharply. His disc sideslipped away from Craig.

The next instant the Earthman was flying through the air, jerked clear of his carrier by the whiplash.

Dimly, he heard Narla scream.

Then he was swinging free, like a plumb bob on it string. Cold sweat drenched him. He clutched at the whiplash, clinging to it with both hands.

Now the disc from which he hung climbed in slow spirals, circling away from the village. Behind and below him Craig glimpsed Narla, similarly suspended, swinging pendulum-like below a second saucer.

The other discs drew in, grouping about the captives in loose formation. Still climbing, the whole flight topped the crest of the hills behind the village.

Here browsed a great herd of the animals Craig had seen grazing. Sweeping low over them, the discs wheeled towards a log stockade atop a knoll, hovered above it for a moment, and then settled slowly.

AT last Craig's feet touched ground inside the stockade. Shaking, he sank to the grass, fumbling to free his wrist from the whiplash.

It came free. Scrambling up, he stumbled to where Narla lay in a crumpled, sobbing heap, and tugged loose the lash that held her.

She clung to him, sobbing, her whole body shaking.

Overhead, the discs still hovered almost motionless, making no move to land.

Anger flared in Craig. Instead of releasing the whip, he surged up suddenly, jerking on it with all his might.

The disc from which Narla had been suspended tilted sharply. The whip-man pitched off, arms flailing, and sprawled spread-eagled in the grass.

Craig dived onto him before he could even catch his breath—pinning him, grasping at his throat.

But already the other discs were plummeting. Sinewy, work-worn hands dragged Craig back.

Then a bronzed young giant who wore a high ceremonial helmet that must once have belonged to some baron's guard came striding forward. "Hold, friend!" He was laughing.

Craig stared. "Bukal!"

"No other." The strapping Baemae gripped Craig's hand.

"But—the guards—I thought you dead."

"And so did I, for a while, there." Bukal chuckled. "But perhaps the gods have marked me to die in the pit with Vydys' rollers. For at the last moment somebody stumbled and I made it away through the alleys, found a new disc, and fled south, here, to my home village."

"So I see." Craig shook his head dazedly.

"As for you, just now, you were not recognized in time." The Baemae was suddenly apologetic. "You'll not begrudge it that we protect our village? After all, the barons have tried a hundred tricks to trap us—so now we bring all strangers here for scrutiny before we pass them on to full fellowship among us."

"Of course not." Craig matched the other's grin. "But is this..." He gestured to the log walls. "...much of a prison?"

Bukal smiled grimly. Leading Craig to the nearest crevice, he pointed out between the logs. "The djevoda stand guard for us."

"The djevoda—?" Craig peered out.

They were strange creatures. Taller than two men they towered—heavy-bodied, six-legged, elephantine. Great tusks gleamed below broad, pig-like snouts.

"Watch!" Bukal commanded.

He drew an ornate dagger from his belt-harness as he spoke. Catching the sun in its jewels, he flashed a beam into the eyes of one of the creatures.

It was as if it were a signal. A roar like that of a maddened bull burst from the djevoda's great throat. Tiger-fast, avalanchal, it lunged up the slope of the knoll, straight for the stockade. The logs rocked under the impact of its hurtling body. A great tusk tore through a crack, bare inches from Craig's arm.

The Earthman leaped back, cursing.

His bronzed friend laughed again. "A wonderful creature, the djevoda. Tons of solid meat, ready for the slicing. But definitely not to be domesticated."

"So I see," Craig agreed, a trifle sourly.

"They charge movement on sight," his guide went on. "Killing them, save from directly above, takes a deal of doing. So, they roam these southern plains by hundreds. That's why this range was never settled, till Tumek gave the flying disc to the Baemae. But overhead, we're safe from them. We can herd them with our whips like cattle, or kill them at will with a bolt at the base of the brain. They feed us, clothe us, protect us, give us freedom…" He broke off. "But I talk too much of our own affairs. Tell me, how did you escape—and what of Tumek?"

Craig said, "Tumek…is dead."

The laughter left the bronzed man's face. "Tumek—dead?" He cursed aloud. "How did it happen?"

Briefly, Craig told him the details of Tumek's death and showed him the crystal. He then elaborated, as best he could, about the ourobos.

Only one thing did he leave out…

Narla.

He didn't know why. It made no sense, even to him.

Yet somehow he couldn't bring himself to reveal her lineage or tell how she came to be here, which Craig knew would certainly thrust her into the role of a hostage.

BUKAL was frowning when Craig finished. "There's too much here I don't understand," he grunted. "Ourobos are not of Lysor, but of our sister planet, Xumar—a loathsome, crawling horror beyond man's controlling. Inoculations with a rare oil will repel them, but no one has ever found a way to kill them. If Zenaor was mad enough to bring them here, to Lysor…" He shuddered and left his sentence hanging.

"And the crystal?" Craig displayed it.

Again, the other shook his head. "For all I know, it might as well be nothing but a lamp lens." He straightened, thin-lipped. "But at least we'll make our masters pay for Tumek! This very night!"

Pivoting as he spoke, he strode back towards the waiting discmen. "These two…" He gestured to Craig and Narla. "…they are accepted. Take them to the village."

Only then did it dawn on Craig that the Baemae had asked not a question about the girl.

But there was little time for pondering on that. The men spun their discs then helped both Earthman and girl to board them. The ground, the stockade, fell away.

Then the hills, too, lay behind, and they were gliding down beyond the palisade, into the village.

A withered crone led Craig and Narla to a hut. "Rest here, warrior—you and your woman. Tomorrow will be time enough to think of work and duty."

She left them, then, closing the door behind her as she departed…

Silence echoed through the room. Wordless, Craig turned to leave.

But Narla's voice stopped him, "Wait, Craig Nesom…"

He swung round. "What—?"

She said, "You didn't tell them that I was Zenaor's daughter. You let them believe I was your woman." A note of strain, of puzzlement, crept into her tone. "Why, Earthman? Why?"

Craig shrugged. "What point was there? Did it matter?"

"Yes, Craig." The gray eyes were thoughtful now. "Yes, it matters very much. You brought me here to use as a weapon against my father—yet now you keep my secret. Why?"

Craig shrugged again, not speaking.

"Because Zenaor's daughter would have received a different welcome, Craig; so very different. You know that, surely."

He nodded slowly. "Yes, I knew it."

"Then why—?"

"Because there's been too much of blood and killing." He lashed out the words in sudden fury, out of all proportion. "I wouldn't turn in a dog to be tormented…"

The girl came to him, through the shadows, until she was close…so very close. "Then…it was not for anything that you felt towards me that you saved me?"

She swayed as she spoke—swayed forward, against him. He could feel the slow beat of her heart, the measured pressure of her breathing. The fragrance of her hair rose in his nostrils.

"No," he said. "No. There was nothing."

For a long, long moment she stood still, not moving. Then, very softly, she said, "You lie, Craig Nesom!"

Something inside Craig let go like a taut spring snapping. "Damn you…" he muttered, and crushed her to him, hard against him.

She came willingly, body warm and vibrant; eyes closed, lips parted.

Red lips—softer than any dream of Vydys.

Craig drank deep of them.

Then, at last, the kiss was ended. They stood there, breathing hard, clinging to each other in the semi-darkness;

and Narla said, "They spoke truly, Craig Nesom. I am—will always be—your woman."

He kissed her again, then, while a knot drew tight in his belly, and his throat swelled, and his eyes stung.

But all he could whisper was…

"Narla…Narla…"

Outside, someone knocked on the door.

Craig stiffened; straightened. "What is it?"

"It's me Bukal. Roh's coming up. Would you raid with us?"

Craig looked at Narla.

Pain was in her eyes, but her voice stayed steady, "Your life's your own, voyager. And…I'll be waiting."

Craig called, "I'm coming, Bukal!"

They kissed again, and then he left her, striding out into the pale green light of the ebbing day.

OVER by the disc-shed, men were working—stacking the saucers one upon the other till they formed neat cylinders, each half-a-dozen discs high.

Laughing, bronzed Bukal gestured to them. "You see, Craig? These are our weapons! Why should we kill, when we can hurt the cursed barons worse by sending their serfs through the skies to freedom?"

Craig nodded.

Another man came up. "We're ready, Bukal."

"Good!" The Baemae leader strode to the shed and caught up a disc. "Here. Craig. Lend a hand!"

Following his lead, Craig dragged a single saucer out into the open and spun it till it hovered on the wave-force.

"Now lash it fast atop a unit."

Moving the saucer to the nearest pile, Craig tied it down. A tilt—a shove—and all seven saucers took the air.

A man scrambled aboard each cylinder as it rose.

"North, now!" cried Bukal. "We'll see how the Lady Vydys likes running her estates without the Baemae!"

Vydys—!

Dark loveliness, rising from a dead guard's corpse with her knife still dripping blood.

Craig shuddered.

Only then they were rising, circling, and there was no time for thoughts or shudders. High through the emerald sky they flashed while the hills fell away and the village vanished. Koh's green ball sank from sight beyond the horizon. Roh, climbed afar, tinting Lysor's fields all blue and purple.

And still they raced north, the night wind whipping at hair and garments.

Then, far below, a black line scarred the grasslands. Craig caught a faint shout: "The barrier!"

Again, he was above the land of the Kukzubas barons.

Ahead, the stocky Bukal waved a sweeping signal. Discs slipped earthward.

Another signal. They dropped lower...lower...came at last to ground in the shadow of a grove of great sefopp trees.

Out of the murk, the dim figure of a burly man hurried towards them. "Thank the gods, you've come!"

Craig could see Bukal stiffen. "Why? Is there trouble?"

"Is there anything *but* trouble?" the other shot back, hoarse-voiced. "Someone betrayed your contact man to the Lady Vydys when she arrived back from Torneulan this morning. He died by her own hand in the torture chambers."

Bukal cursed. "Did he talk?"

"Would I be here if he had?" the burly man snarled back. He scrubbed his palms on the front of his loose Baemae tabard. "The others are waiting for me to bring the word of your coming."

"Then get them!"

The burly man vanished into the shadows.

Bukal pivoted back to his helpers. "Hurry! Unlash the saucers!"

In seconds, the cargo of discs was spread out. Already, more men from the estate shuffled from the grove's blackness.

Then the burly man, too, returned. "All here," he grunted.

Bukal shot a quick glance around. "No women—?"

"No." The man shifted. "We thought you'd want fighters."

"Fighters—?" Bukal stiffened. "What do you mean? Why would we need fighters?"

The burly one fumbled. "Why...to meet Zenaor's raiding party."

"Raiders—!"

"Yes. Had you no warning?" The informer choked on his own spittle. "Vydys herself brought the word. Last night an alien from another system stole Zenaor's daughter and disced south with her. Now Zenaor swears—"

Bukal swung round, eyes blazing. "Earthman! Is this true?"

Numbly, Craig nodded.

"That girl! Zenaor's own daughter!" Bukal choked with fury. "You brought her to our village! You gave no warning!"

Craig held his voice chill, "So? Could you ask for a better hostage?"

"No. Not if we had known. But now—" Bukal broke off and whirled round. "You," he said to the burly man, "take your people and head south to protect our village. The rest of us will run the barrier and try to intercept the raiders. As for you, alien." He turned back to Craig, eyes hot and scornful. "You'll go south also. But as prisoner, not one of us."

Craig looked to the others; searched their faces.

Their eyes held no mercy.

"All right, you. Come on!" The burly man started towards Craig.

CRAIG whipped up his fire-gun and laid the barrel hard along the other's temple.

The man slumped to the ground.

Craig said tightly, "To hell with the lot of you! I'm no man's prisoner!"

"Curse you, alien!" Bukal took a quick step forward.

Craig leveled the fire-gun at the flat, bronzed belly.

Bukal halted.

Craig flicked the weapon's muzzle to the nearest of the Baemae. "You! Spin me a disc!"

Seconds stretched to eternity. Then the man's eyes fell. Wordless, he shuffled through the echoing silence, tilted up a disc, and whipped it round.

The magnetic currents caught it; held it, hovering.

Craig vaulted aboard it. "Death's waiting for the man that follows…"

He threw his weight to one side, then back again. Rocking, the saucer swirled upward.

Again he tilted; sent it careening around the far end of the line of trees.

Behind him, Bukal shouted an order. There was a rush of feet, a flurry of movement.

Craig leaned far out, so that the disc almost doubled on its course, sliding back on the other side of the masking sefopp trees. Then, dropping it swiftly back to the ground, he leaped off and dragged it into the shadows.

Saucers sped past the end of the grove, riders and discs alike silhouetted dimly against the blue-black sky. Craig crept deeper into the undergrowth, flat on his belly.

More aching tension. More seconds dragging by, turning into minutes.

Then discs swept down again. Craig heard someone rasp, "He's gone, Bukal. We couldn't spot him." And then Bukal, cursing: "We can't wait any longer. Not with Zenaor prowling."

Again, discs tilted skyward. All of them, this time.

Silence once more, broken only by the whisper of breeze and trees, the chirp of insects.

Craig crept back to his own saucer and wheeled it out into the open. Ten seconds later he, too, was climbing into Lysor's dark night sky.

Climbing—to what end, with every man's hand against him? Bukal or Zenaor, Baemae or barons, one and all sought his blood.

All but Narla.

Somehow, he had to reach her.

Grim, tight-lipped, he set a course southeast, veering just far enough north of the village so that he might pass Vydys' serfs undetected. Their very numbers might slow them. There was at least a bare chance that a lone man might reach Narla ahead of them.

Only then, as he sped on, he caught a sound.

He hesitated, straining his ears.

The noise came again—a muffled, rhythmic clanking.

Craig veered a fraction; raced towards the sound.

BELOW Craig, dots appeared against the blue-gray shimmer of the grasslands—dots that crawled grimly, steadily southward.

He knew, then—knew what the dots meant, and the clanking. A chill ran through him.

These were heavy vehicles in motion! This was Zenaor's column, grinding towards the village. They'd passed the barrier far ahead of Bukal.

And Vydys' serfs would never stand a chance against their power, their numbers.

That left it up to him.

Only what could one man do?

Cursing, Craig circled far ahead of the raiders—searching the rolling hills below, praying for some miracle of terrain, some inspiration.

But no miracle came. There were only the grasslands, the great straggling herds of the djevoda.

The djevoda—!

Craig came up short. Here was his miracle. Here his allies. Sideslipping his disc in a flashing are, he surveyed the ground beyond the column.

The vehicles were following the low ground, moving towards a pass of sorts in the hills that sprawled east and west across their path.

Craig raced south again. A long way south, till at last he passed above the distant range and swept down on its far side.

How long did he have? An hour? Or only half that?

A knot of djevoda moved restlessly as his disc's shadow fell across them.

Craig slashed back closer.

Rumbling their irritation, the huge, ungainly beasts turned west, drifting towards the pass.

Craig searched out another, larger group and turned it, too. Then another. Another.

Across the hills, Zenaor's column was creeping closer. Sweat rolled down Craig's back. He crowded his growing herd of djevoda harder.

The beasts were angry now—bellowing their rage through the stillness of the night; lunging at him, tusks high, when he swept too close.

If he should slip or fall—! He shuddered.

Then the first of the creatures began to funnel into the mouth of the pass. Craig raced his saucer back, moving up others to press in behind the leaders.

Now, again, the clanking of Zenaor's carriers drifted to Craig. He maneuvered his disc in a tight spiral—climbing, climbing.

The grasslands fell away below him. The range spread out like a problem in tactics set on a sand table, here were the djevoda, straggling into the pass. Beyond the hills, Zenaor's column twisted towards them, snake-like, as if hastening to join battle.

Already, the lead vehicles were swinging south into the rift.

Craig plummeted down ahead of the first djevoda.

Roaring, they fell back.

The Earthman raced away in a monstrous circle—driving in the beasts, crowding them together in a milling herd that numbered hundreds.

The column was in the pass now, hurrying forward faster, as if its commanders realized the danger of such close quarters.

Craig rounded up the last straggling djevoda and hovered just above and beyond them, waiting.

DOWN the pass, lights gleamed. Drifting dust set Craig to coughing. The rumble and clanking echoed like distant thunder.

Craig dropped to one knee on his disc; brought out his fire-gun.

The approaching lights shone brighter. A beam sprayed across the first of the djevoda.

The creatures' great, tusked snout-heads lowered. Huge feet churned up choking clouds of dust.

Craig held his breath.

The lead carrier rocked over a bump. Metal clanged on metal. The lights flashed into the djevodas' eyes.

It was a signal. With a deafening roar, a djevoda lunged forward.

The carrier's brakes screamed.

But already the mountainous beast was thundering down upon it. Like an avalanche of flesh and bone, it crashed into the vehicle. Screams clashed with the shriek of rending metal. Craig blazed with the fire-gun at the packed, elephantine mass of animated death below him.

Bellowing with rage and pain, the whole herd swept forward—on into the pass, following the already-charging leaders.

More carriers braked and crashed into each other.

Then the herd was upon them, smashing at them. Green fire seared through the night, mingling with the crashing thunder of some other, heavier weapon. Craig glimpsed a djevoda torn asunder in mid-stride, its six massive legs gone suddenly limp and sprawling.

But no human power could stop that hurtling, murderous tidal wave of flesh. Through the whole column the djevodas raged—crushing carriers, overturning them, stomping them to masses of shapeless metal.

At the far end of the pass, the last of the vehicles wheeled about in blind, desperate haste. Engines roaring, they raced for the safety of the open grasslands.

Only then, flashing shapes lanced down out of the skies to the north. Men dropped from discs onto carrier-tops, clamping their capes across the vision-slits.

Vehicles ground to a halt. Crews stumbled out, hands high in panic and surrender.

Craig surged to his feet; sent his own disc climbing.

Too late. For now saucers hung above him, too, hemming him in from all directions...saucers ridden by Bukal's lean, bronzed raiders.

And there was Bukal.

"Craig...friend—!" he shouted. "Hold, Craig Nesom!"

Craig stood rigid atop his disc.

But then the other was beside him, waving and laughing. "Can you forgive me, Craig? Without this blow you've struck, without the firing-sounds to guide us, we'd never have caught up with this column."

"And...Narla—?"

Bukal swept the whole sky with his waving gesture. "Go to her, Earthman! After this night's work I'd even give you Zenaor!"

He signaled as he spoke. The discs above Craig moved aside.

His throat all at once too tight to speak, Craig waved back and spiraled his own disc upward.

But as he did so, another saucer swept down—a saucer ridden by a woman he'd never seen before—a woman with an anguished, strain-straut face. "Alien!" Her voice broke ragged. "Where is Bukal?"

"Here, T'clar!" He glided up beside her. "What is it? Is there trouble?"

"The village—" Again her voice broke, and for a moment Craig thought she was going to faint. Then, rallying, she burst out, "Bukal, the men from the estate of Lady Vydys—"

"Yes, T'clar—?"

"They were her guards, not of the Baemae."

A numb horror gripped Craig. He hardly heard the rush of words between them.

But…he had to know.

He blurted, "The woman who was with me—Narla—"

And then, the answer: "Alien, it was she they came for. Now they are gone again—and she is with them!"

CHAPTER SIX

MORNING. Pale green morning, and the vast estate of dark Vydys the Cruel.

Bukal begged, "Give it up, Craig Nesom. There is no hope. Besides, this is between the Kukzubas, the barons. Vydys seized your Narla only as a weapon against Lord Zenaor. She will not harm her."

Craig cursed him.

The bronzed Baemae's lips drew thin. "What would you have us do, then, alien? Throw our discs against her defenses? Gut ourselves on her guards' weapons?"

Bleakly, Craig stared up at the shining ramparts. Bitterness seethed in him.

And yet...was it his right to be bitter? These were brave men, dedicated to the Baemae's fight against the barons. But Narla was not of them. The things she meant to him lay between two only.

He said, "Forgive me, Bukal. You and your people—you have troubles enough. I could not give you more."

"Then what—?"

"I'll go alone."

The hot light left Bukal's eyes. He gripped the Earthman's arm. "No, Craig—"

"Yes, Bukal." Craig pulled free of the other's hand.

"But—"

But Craig was weary of argument, of empty phrases. Tilting his disc, he raced away from the Baemae leader, skimming out as the swallow swoops, straight for the gates of Vydys' shaft-like Tower of Cadilek.

But green fire blazed from the port-slots. Veering sharply, Craig sped away again, climbing along the wall in the shelter of the angle bastion.

Then he had topped the lowest level's battlements. Leveling off, he glided across the roof to a point beyond the central obelisk where none could see him.

There, at last, he brought his disc to rest.

But no attack from above would baffle Vydys. Not after that night of blood of Torneulan.

Ignoring the roof-ports, Craig crossed quickly to the parapet along the rear wall. A coil of rope, stripped from his waist, gave him a line down. In seconds he was upon the ground.

Fire-gun in hand, then, he moved along the wall to a deep-set, shrubbery-shrouded postern.

The door opened at his first pressure. A dim-lit, stonewalled corridor loomed, inviting.

An invitation to death, perhaps…

Cat-footed, Craig slipped inside…stood taut and breathless, waiting.

But no sound came, no sign of guards or trouble.

Craig's scalp prickled. This was too easy.

But trap or not, here lay his only chance at Vydys, his only hope of reaching Narla.

Shadow-silent, he moved down the hallway to twin kresh-wood doors, one set on each side of the passage.

Craig pressed each in turn. But they were locked; they would not budge.

Raw-nerved, he moved on again.

Now came a short stair, leading down. At the bottom, a heavy door barred the passage.

Walking softly, the Earthman descended—then reached for the door.

IT swung wide before he even touched it. Light blazed, so bright he fell back a step, half-blinded. A voice said, "Welcome, Craig Nesom…"

The voice of Vydys.

Craig pivoted.

But now, behind him, the kresh-wood doors had opened. Guards stood at the ready, weapons poised.

Craig faced the light again.

It shone like a dazzling wall. Even shielding his eyes, Craig could see nothing for its brilliance.

Vydys' voice commanded, "Come forward, alien. I would not harm you."

He sucked in a breath and stepped across the threshold.

Hands shot out…seized him…held him helpless while they wrenched away his fire-gun and his dagger.

Then, incredibly, Vydys was saying, "Away, guards! Leave us." And he was free again and stumbling forward, the door slamming shut behind him.

Groping, he drew himself erect. Then he turned, searching for the woman.

But still there was only the blazing silver light, dazzling him to blindness. Her laughter rippled out of nowhere, a sound to sting him to rising fury.

He lashed out, "How long do I stand here, woman? Do you fear to face me?"

"Fear you—?" She laughed again, and now there was a new note in her voice, an element he could not name or place. "No, warrior, I do not fear you."

Even as she spoke, the dazzling light was fading. Like a wall dissolving, the veil of its brilliance fell away.

Vydys stood before Craig, high on a dais.

Blinking, he stared up at her.

The ripe lips curved into a smile. Sinuous, cat-graceful, she moved towards him, a sleek silvery body sheath shimmering as she descended. "You see, Earthman? I told you I did not fear you."

He stared down into the midnight eyes, black and unfathomable as the void itself. "Then what——?"

The scarlet lips parted. She swayed against him. "Kiss me, alien…"

Involuntarily, Craig stiffened. "What——!"

The woman laughed softly. "Is it so strange a concept, alien? Am I so old, so drab, so ugly?"

Craig could find no words.

"We are as one in so many ways, Craig Nesom," Dark Vydys went on. "Fear is not in us, nor yet mercy. We know what it means to strike with daring. Both of us hold ruthless to our hatred for Lord Zenaor."

Still Craig did not move. "And because we both hate Zenaor, I should kiss you?"

"If we stand together, we can defeat him." The dark eyes half mocked, half measured. "Some say that pain is my only passion. That is not true. I love also as a woman. There are men, Kukzubas barons, who would sell their souls for my embrace."

"Then why not give it?"

"Why——?" The throaty laughter rippled. "Because they desire me does not mean I want them, Earthling. I seek a man of blood and iron as well as passion—a champion to aid me against Zenaor."

In spite of himself, Craig smiled thinly. "Some might call that a tribute. To me, it seems left-handed."

Vydys frowned, ever so slightly. "I do not understand you, alien. Would it be such punishment to sit beside me, ruling Lysor?" And then, eager again: "For we can do it, with your valor and the weapon they say you received from the one called Tumek."

"The weapon—"

"Yes. A crystal, to win power even over the Xumuian ourobos my spies say Zenaor plans to use against the Baemae. You have it, do you not?"

SHE drew closer as she spoke. Her hands slid over him and touched the jewel case where it lay flat against his body. Before he could stop her, she had it out and open.

"So... This is the thing! A pretty bauble..."

Craig didn't answer.

"How do you use it, alien?"

"I don't know."

"You don't know..." The smooth face stiffened. "Or...is it that you won't tell me?"

Craig shrugged. "Have it as you want it."

For an instant the woman's nostrils flared. Then, once again, she was close to him—her breasts, her body, smooth and firm against him. "Please, Earthman! Do not make me believe that you are one of those who can love no woman!"

Craig held his silence.

A flush came to Vydys' dark, lovely face. She stepped back, eyes bright with anger. "Is it another, then—that blonde hag, Narla?"

Craig's fists clenched. His shoulders stiffened.

"It is, then! You'd scorn me for her?" Vydys' scarlet lips peeled back. "Very well. You shall have her—as soon as you give me the secret of the crystal..."

Sweat came to Craig Nesom's forehead. "I can't tell you what I don't know."

"You leave me little choice, then." Vydys was almost purring. "I must have protection against Zenaor and his ourobos. Unless you share the crystal's secret with me, I shall be forced to sell the wench back to her father for the tanagree oil that would drive off the slime monsters."

Dry-lipped, Craig said, "So be it."

"But I had such pleasant fantasies of how I would amuse myself with her in my torture chambers." Vydys' eyes grew wide and doleful. "There are so many things that one can try. And a young, nubile girl may live for hours…"

Craig bit down hard to keep from shuddering.

"But since you will not help me," Vydys sighed, turned, walked up the dais. "At least, your death shall entertain my favorites."

Craig would have lunged for her, then.

But she struck a great gong sharply. Instantly, the dazzling light-wall blazed forth to shield her. Guards leaped from nowhere to seize the Earthman. Their blows made his head ring.

"To the pit with him!" Vydys cried shrilly. "To the pit!"

Craig's world resolved into a nightmare of dank corridors and blows and blackness.

Then, suddenly, he was in the open once again, tottering on the rim of a deep, walled trench that ran about a side-shaft of the Vydys' tower like a sort of moat.

"Look down, alien!"

Blear-eyed, Craig stared down into the pit.

Great tusks speared up at him. The bellow of an enraged djevoda rang in his ears.

Vydys said, "You and your Baemae friends are said to be clever with these creatures, alien. Especially with a whip." She turned to one of her retinue. "Give him the lash."

The man brought out a long Baemae whip and handed it to Craig.

"Down with him!"

In seconds, Craig swung into the moat at the end of a rope-loop.

He was still staggering when the djevoda charged, thundering its rage.

Craig lashed out with the whip. But without avail. The stinging lash brought a new roar of fury from the great creature. Savagely, it lunged again.

BARELY in time, Craig leaped out of the way. Desperately, he ran through the trench in search of some exit, some chance for escape.

There was none.

Again the djevoda charged.

Once more Craig sidestepped in the nick of time.

Above him, on the pit's rim, Vydys laughed her silvery, sadistic laugh.

Hate surged through the Earthman…hate mingled with fear.

Was he to die here—tusked high into the air; trampled under the great hammer-like feet?

If at least the she-beast above only could die with him—!

He fell back to the moat's far edge—but not at the djevoda. No. Higher, this time. Higher—and straight at Vydys!

The long lash slashed through the air. Almost lazily, it seemed—it drifted. The snapper lifted…curled…wrapped round Vydys' slim waist.

She screamed, then.

Too late. Because now Craig was surging back on the whipstock with all his strength, a savage jerk.

The woman lurched forward, across the parapet. Down the steep face she slid, straight into the trench.

Along the rim, tumult erupted. Guards shouted. Serfs raced this way and that. Fire-guns blazed down at the djevoda. A ladder appeared, shoved down from above.

Dropping the whipstock, Craig lunged for the ladder.

A guard was scrambling down it. Catching him from behind, Craig knocked him sprawling to the side. When another head appeared above the parapet, Craig butted low, not slowing.

Blood—blows—violence. A race for the postern. As from afar, Craig caught the echo of Vydys' scream: "The alien! Stop him!"

So she still lived...

More guards. Veering, Craig darted through the nearest door and pounded through a maze of echoing corridors and stairways.

If only he could reach the roof, his saucer...

Locked doors. Dead-end hallways. Men racing towards him.

Craig sprinted toward a window.

Below lay the outer grounds.

Craig leaped.

As he did so, a familiar shadow swooped low—the shadow of a disc.

Bukal. He brought the disc down in a fast sideslip. "Quick—!"

Craig dived onto the saucer.

Then they were climbing—up, away from Vydys' Tower of Cadilek, away from guards and clenched fists and shouted imprecations.

Still panting, Craig said, "That was close, Bukal. Thanks."

Bukal didn't answer.

Craig craned round, peered up at him. "Bukal! What's the matter?"

His bronzed face stayed bleak and bitter, his eyes watery with emotion. "It's the end, Earthman," he answered heavily. "Do you hear me? It's the end of my people. The end of our quest for freedom."

"The end—?" Staring, Craig fought down a numbness. "You don't mean—?"

"Yes." Bukal's slash-mouth twisted. "Zenaor has carried out his threat. In a hundred spots south of the barrier, the ourobos are unleashed against us!"

CHAPTER SEVEN

RESTLESSLY, the djevodas lumbered through the grasslands—a large herd, numbering over half a hundred.

A tension seemed to hang about the creatures. Great snout-heads lifted as if sniffing the morning breeze, then lowered again, swinging to and fro, watchful and surly.

"You see?" Bukal clipped. "They sense that today they are the hunted, not the hunters."

Frowning, Craig nodded.

"Come now. The nearest of the places we seek is farther south."

Craig tilted his disc, following Bukal as the Baemae leader skimmed his own saucer away, high above the ranges.

Below them, another herd appeared. Another.

Bukal shouted, "Observe, Craig Nesom! They move north—all of them!"

The Earthmen stared. Bukal's words were true. The scene below was like some vast migration, a sudden shift that turned the behemoths ever northward towards the barrier that separated this free land from the tyranny of the Kuk-zubas barons.

Too, these new herds were moving faster, hardly pausing to tusk up the rich roots on which the monsters fed.

They crossed a river. Bukal drifted his disc in close to Craig's. "Watch, now. From here on we may find ourobos."

Even as he spoke, a wild scream of rage, of terror, rose from a distant group of the djevoda.

"Quick—!" Bukal raced ahead.

Craig followed, sweeping low behind him.

Then they were above the monstrous sextupeds—hovering, peering. Craig glimpsed gray movement amidst the green-gold grass-clumps...a shimmering as of slime that crawled and eddied. He started to glide lower.

"No—!" Bukal cried. "Stop, Craig! Don't chance it!"

There could be no mistaking the urgency of his tone. Discing higher, Craig studied the ground below in careful detail.

Now it dawned on him that more than one gray splotch showed. Here lay another; there, two more. Like water, they seemed to seep across the land in slithering tendrils.

The djevodas were bunching now, crowding together. Their great feet hammered at the earth. They tusked up clods in sudden furies.

Bukal hung close. "You see? They are surrounded." His voice was bitter.

It was true. Everywhere, gray patches hemmed in the djevoda. While Craig watched, they linked and joined, eddying together...grew larger, larger, till they lay on the range like a sodden, ever-spreading blanket.

The djevodas stomped and pawed. Rage echoed in their roaring bellows...rage, and something more, something close akin to panic.

The gray took on new thickness. As if feeding on the very air itself, it piled in glistening layers.

THEN, rippling in Boh's green glow, a tendril crept from the mass, slithering through the grass towards the djevodas.

Slowly...slowly...

It touched a great foot...curled about the ankle.

Still unaware, the djevoda started to turn.

The slime swirled about the foot—clinging, holding.

The djevoda's bellow went shrill with terror. Aware of the danger now, it lunged savagely.

The foot tore free.

But now panic was upon the giant sextuped. Roaring, it charged across the clear space, straight into the mass of circling gray.

Its fellows followed.

Like a hideous gray wave, the slime swept in upon them— miring them, surging high onto their lumbering bodies.

The djevodas screamed and slashed and struggled.

But it was as if they were wallowing in quicksand. Each lunge, each tusk-slash, only brought the gray tide rolling higher. Splattering, each gray patch grew as it touched its quarry. In bare seconds the wave-thing engulfed the struggling giants.

The last scream died, swallowed up in the gray death of the ourobos. Folds of slime rippled over final, paroxysmal spasms.

Shuddering. Craig whipped his disc into a tight, climbing spiral. The breeze was suddenly chill upon him, and he retched till his quivering stomach emptied.

Grim-faced, Bukal hovered beside him. "A pretty picture, is it not?"

Craig couldn't answer.

"So it goes everywhere across the grasslands. Like a tide, the ourobos sweep over the south, pausing and gathering only long enough to kill, then spreading out once more in ever-greater numbers…" His voice trailed off…

"But—is there nothing—?"

"Nothing that will stop them? No." Bukal's jaw jutted, hard and angry. "No, Craig. Nothing. Our people learned that long ago, on Xumar, the ourobos' home planet. Tanagree oil injections will render man distasteful to them;

otherwise even the barons' military stations there would have had to be abandoned."

"Then—the oil—"

"They do not like it; that is all. It doesn't harm them."

"Oh."

"Already, our villages are emptying. By tomorrow the whole of the free Baemae will be crowded close along the border. The day after—who knows?"

Craig frowned. "Tumek thought he had an answer."

Bukal's face didn't change. "Tumek lies in his grave, and Vydys holds his crystal." His bitterness ate like acid.

Craig had no words. Silently, he stared away, off across the rolling southern grasslands.

Was there no solution anywhere to this monstrous scheme of Zenaor's? Would other planets go down before it like the Baemae? And his own life...must he resign himself to defeat and death? Was that to be his destiny, the end of his assignment here on Lysor?

Bleakly, he wondered.

Then, afar off, a moving speck appeared, racing through the sky. Craig stiffened. "Bukal..."

The Baemae shaded his eyes. "A disc," he clipped, tight-lipped. "More trouble..."

Together, Lysorian and Earthman lanced towards the approaching saucer.

Then it was close at hand, and Craig could hardly believe his eyes. For a woman rode it—a slim, young girl with golden hair that rippled and shimmered in the sunlight.

"Narla—!" he choked. "Narla!"

She swept close, then, and they grounded their discs on a knoll and she was in his arms again, laughing and crying at once.

PUSHING her back at last, Craig held her at arm's length, feasting his eyes upon her. For today she was a different Narla. Her heavy Kukzubas cape was gone, replaced by the scanty scarlet halter and paneled belt of the free Baemae. A fire-gun hung at her hip, a jeweled ceremonial dagger across her thigh, and she carried one of the long black whips with which Bukal's men herded the djevoda.

Laughing, she pirouetted. "You see, Craig? This time I come as one of you, not Zenaor's kidnapped daughter."

Craig nodded. "Yes, I see. But—what of your father? How did you get here?"

A shadow crossed the lovely face. But the girl's gray eyes stayed clear, her voice steady, "Once, Craig Nesom, I told you that I was—would ever be—your woman. That is what brought me here—that only. My father took me from Vydys, yes, trading tanagree oil for my life. But he could not hold me. Not when you stood here, fighting with the Baemae. I fled from the Central Tower to an old friend among the Baemae. She gave me this garb and saucer, and told me where to find you. So, now..." She shrugged smooth shoulders. "...I am here, to stand beside you."

Wordless, unable to speak, Craig again embraced her.

Only then Bukal was talking, breaking in upon them. "The ourobos come closer," he clipped. "There's no time to waste. My people need me."

Spinning their discs, the three took to the air and ranged north till they reached the river and the village.

The village. Tension crawled through it now, lined on every face, reflected in every movement. Men, women, children—they crowded round as the trio stepped from their discs.

Bukal searched the frightened faces. "What is it?"

"New nests of ourobos!" a man burst out; and another croaked, "Already, the djevodas are in flight. By tonight—"

He broke off. There was no need to say more.

"Then...we have no choice." Bukal shrugged, bronzed shoulders heavy. "We must join the others along the barrier."

"Must we?" This from a woman. "Must we, Bukal—when we hold Zenaor's daughter as our prisoner?"

Taut silence echoed, sudden as summer thunder.

Frowning, Bukal looked down at the speaker. "What nonsense—?" he began.

But a man shoved forward and cut in upon him. "No nonsense, Bukal!" he flashed fiercely. "All morning, the amplifiers have been blaring across the barrier. Zenaor says he'll leave us free, safe from the ourobos, in trade for this wench and her alien lover!"

More echoing silence. More vibrant tension.

Then Bukal snapped, "Enough of this drivel! Zenaor's daughter or not, this girl's cast her lot with us. As for Craig Nesom—"

From one side, a rawboned, ape-like discman smashed a blow to the back of Bukal's head. The leader spilled to the ground.

Like wolves, the crowd surged forward.

Craig drove a fist into the face of the man who'd struck Bukal; lashed a kick to the groin of another, beside him.

Then green fire blazed, a blast that seared between him and the Baemae.

The crowd stopped short; fell back.

Fire-gun in hand, bronzed body glistening, Bukal lurched to his feet. Blood dripped from his earlobe. "You scum, would you buy your lives with treason?"

No one moved. No one spoke.

"Craig..."

The Earthman shifted to his friend's side in one quick movement. "Yes, Bukal."

The Baemae chief's eyes stayed on the crowd, his finger tight on the fire-gun's trigger. Face a bleak, expressionless mask, he said, "I see that I can no longer control my people. But at least you need not suffer for it. Take Narla and go!"

Wordless, Craig nodded. The girl beside him, he backed to the nearest discs.

THE Baemae fell back before him. He could feel their eyes on his back as he spun the saucers. Their hate surged over him like the magnetic waves on which the discs lifted.

Into the air again, rising…passing over palisades and circling hills, racing away northwest towards the barons' barrier.

Where could they go? What would they do?

Bleakly, Craig mulled dark thoughts. He was glad that she kept her own council, till he saw her brush at her eyes and knew she was crying.

Yet what solace could anyone offer her in this nightmare?

Now other villages passed below them. Grey folds ringed one, glistening in Yoh's white light as they closed in upon it.

Craig closed his ears to the screams of the doomed and sent his disc hurtling faster.

Then the black line of the barrier loomed ahead. The blare of amplifiers rose faintly.

Craig turned. "Hover here awhile, while I reconnoiter."

Mutely, Narla nodded. He sped away.

More villages, more djevoda, more gray patches. The amplifiers, bellowing: "Bring in my daughter, Baemae! Bring in my daughter and the alien!"

No refuge.

Craig circled back.

Only now, two discs swayed where one had hung before. And one was sweeping down on the other.

On Narla.

Craig whipped his own saucer higher, and then higher.

A man in high-fronted metal helmet rode the second disc, the one that was gliding down towards the girl. While Craig watched, he swung out his long black djevoda whip…tilted his disc till it plummeted like a speeding arrow.

Craig raced towards them.

Now Narla, too, saw the stranger. She tried to tilt her saucer.

But the man in the helmet pancaked his disc down, level…swung the whip. The lash curled round Narla's wrist.

She jerked back in a panic. Tottered.

Then her disc tilted and she was sliding…falling…

Craig careened his own carrier down.

The stranger's head came round. He clawed for the fire-gun in his belt-holster.

Craig shifted sharply. His disc's edge dropped. Before Narla's attacker could twist or duck, the edge hit him.

He bounced backward, out into empty air, flailing wildly. The handle of his whip sang by Craig's head.

With a desperate lunge, the Earthman caught it…clung to it while Narla swung in a wide arc beneath him.

The stranger's scream died in the thud of his body striking.

Sweat-drenched, gasping, Craig maneuvered his own disc down till Narla's feet were on the ground once more. Another moment and he was stumbling to her, hugging her shaking body to his. "My darling…my darling…"

How long did they stand so? An hour? A minute?

Only then, at last, they were no longer shaking. Once more, Craig could taste her lips and smell her fragrance and feel the softness of her hair as it rippled like ripe rangeland grasses.

But with that consciousness came other things—a far-off scream…a panic-straut knot of djevoda, fleeing…the faint, rank distant scent of the ourobos.

Away, beyond the barrier, the amplifier bellowed, "Give up my daughter, Baemae! Give up my daughter and the alien!"

NARLA'S cheek was soft against Craig's…softer than any satin. He kissed her eyes…tasted the salt of the tears that welled from them.

His Narla, crying.

Again the amplifier roared its message: "Give up my daughter, Baemae! That is the price of life! Give up my daughter and the alien!"

Bleakly, Craig turned and looked back across the grasslands.

No longer were they a serfman's refuge. Not now. Not with the ourobos' slime upon them.

A flurry of movement caught his eye. Faintly, he heard djevoda bellow panic.

The panic that came with the ourobos. The same kind that turned free Baemae into wolves, hunting down his Narla.

"If you do not give them up, I'll know my daughter's dead and you will die with her!" the amplifier shrieked. "Give her up, Baemae! Give her up and live! Why should you care what happens to the alien, Nesom?"

Why indeed?

Tight-lipped, Craig pivoted.

His thoughts must have shown on his face, or in his eyes. Narla clung to him—gray eyes tear-filled, lips aquiver. "No, Craig! No!"

He held her to him for a moment.

Hoarse shouts. Djevoda screaming. Rippling eddies, gray and obscene, amid the green-gold of the grasslands.

"Give them up, Baemae! Give them up or die!"

Craig said, "It doesn't matter, Narla. Not really. I've fought and I've lost, and a man has to play the cards fate deals him. But there's no reason for the others, the Baemae, to die with me. Not if there's even the slimmest chance for them to live if I surrender. As for you, your father wants you back, that's all. He'll never harm you."

She was still sobbing as he lifted her onto the saucer…

CHAPTER EIGHT

THE Central Tower of Torneulan, the Tower of Zenaor. Hard-faced guards. Echoing passageways. The bleak metal and leather of Zenaor's private chambers.

And Zenaor.

The Lord Zenaor, high chief of all Kukzubas barons.

The lean face was set in cruel lines now, the jet eyes narrowed to black diamonds beneath their heavy brows.

"So, alien…" His voice rasped, thick with menace. "At last you come to me, begging for mercy—"

"Mercy? From you?" Craig Nesom shrugged in spite of the guards' restraining hands, the shackles. "No, Zenaor. I beg nothing of you, neither life nor lenience. The things I've done I'd do again. I've given up only to stop this senseless slaughter."

"An altruistic gesture, alien," Zenaor chuckled. "But a trifle late."

He rose as he spoke and stepped to a paneled wall behind his seat. A carved section slid back at his touch, revealing a bleak, compact laboratory chamber.

A transparent, closet-sized cubicle stood on a stand in the compartment's center…a cubicle whose every inch and crack and crevice seethed and eddied with the swirling gray slime of ourobos.

In spite of himself, Craig Nesom stiffened; caught the whisper of Narla's quick-drawn breath.

Zenaor pivoted, still chuckling. "You see, alien? Here we have ourobos!"

Craig nodded slowly.

"And what is the ourobos?" Zenaor was gloating now, caught up in the excitement of his own revelation. "It is what your science would term a thallophyte, Earthman—a semi-intelligent thallophyte, a sort of deadly, highly-mobile fungus for which no specific has been discovered!"

"A fungus—!"

"Yes, alien! That's why no weapon prevails against it! Blast it, even with fire, and still asexual spores fly out, each to form the nucleus for another of its kind, a new ourobos!"

Craig's lips were dry. His voice shook. "Then—this planet, Lysor—"

"Lysor is doomed, you mean?" Triumph rang in the chief barons' voice. "Indeed it is, alien! Now that I've brought the ourobos from Xumar, nothing can stop them! Your sacrifice is wasted! There's barely enough tanagree oil to treat a handful of our barons!"

Craig choked. "No, Zenaor! Not even you could doom a whole race—"

But Zenaor still was speaking, "This is my answer to the free Baemae, Earthman! They wanted Lysor—they shall have it! As for the rest of us—my friends among the Kukzubas, a few loyal serfmen—I have ships already ramped to take us off to Odak, third planet of our system."

Craig stood numb, unable to move or speak.

So now, at last, he knew the truth—the secret behind Zenaor's dark dream of conquest.

Only now was too late. Now was a nonexistent second between the moment of the chief of barons' flight and the time when he'd lay down his challenge to a hundred, a thousand, other planets, backed by the horrid, devastating threat of the ourobos.

And Narla—

SLOWLY, desolately, Craig turned to look at her...to see again the helpless anguish stamped on her lovely, horror-blanched face.

"Now you look to my daughter for solace, Earthman?" Again, it was Zenaor speaking. "You seek to drown the bitterness of death and failure in the knowledge that she, at least, will live because you came in and surrendered?"

New tendrils fluttered in Craig Nesom's belly. He swung back; stared at his lean, merciless captor.

"Shall I tell you more, alien, another thing you did not know?" The chief of barons bared his teeth in a grin that belonged on a bleaching skull. He leaned forward, voice dropping lower, "Though I raised her as such, Narla is not my daughter..."

The very walls rang with shock. Even the cold-eyed guards went rigid.

Zenaor said, "Her father was of the Baemae, alien—and I lusted after the Baemae wife who bore his daughter, Narla. So I slew him, and took wife and child alike into my harem."

"Father—Zenaor..." Narla's poise was cracking.

Ruthlessly, the other pressed on, "She is not of my blood, alien. No ties coerce me to forgive her treason. So she dies here with you—with you and all my enemies, Baemae or baron!"

A madness seized Craig Nesom. Savagely, he hurled himself at his tormentor.

But the guards were too quick, too strong. Brutally, they jerked him back.

He writhed helpless, raging.

Only then a voice—a woman's voice, low and gentle as the hiss of the asp is gentle, "Your enemies, Zenaor—like me, perhaps?"

Craig went rigid. The guards, too—Zenaor, Narla.

A hanging moved aside. Dark Vydys the Cruel stood framed in a doorway—fire-gun in hand, liveried warriors behind her.

"*Vydys*—!" Zenaor's color was draining.

The woman laughed softly. "Surely, my lord, my coming does not surprise you? By way of a test, I injected some of the fluid you gave me into a serfman, then sent him out to meet the ourobos. But they swallowed him up as they would any other, so I came here to discuss it." Airily, she gestured. "Of course, there was some small difficulty with your men at the gates. My troops had to slay them—"

Zenaor sucked in air.

Vydys said, "Your plans for the spaceships—they please me. The fleet shall blast for Odak according to schedule." A pause. A cat's smile. "Of course, you'll not be with it. It's better that you stay here with the Baemae."

"Vydys, in the name of our ancestors—our common blood as Kukzubas—"

"I remember it, Zenaor. You shall not stand unprotected. Vydys brought a flat object from beneath her waist-cape, tossed it onto a table. "Here. I leave you this weapon."

It was the jewel-box that held Tumek's crystal.

Zenaor's fists clenched. "Curse you, Vydys—!"

She turned away as if he had not spoken. Smiling at Craig, she purred, "A last chance for you, Earthling. Would you join me?"

Craig's eyes met Narla's. Then, quietly, he said, "You know my answer, Vydys."

Her face contorted. "Die, then, you fool!"

She started to turn back to Zenaor.

Only then, incredibly, a fire-gun was in his hand, too, whipping up from beneath his scarlet cloak.

They fired together.

Vydys screamed in the same instant. For the fraction of a second green flame seemed to envelope her. A great black char-scar spread across her naked belly.

She tottered. Her guards lunged forward.

But already Zenaor was leaping into the laboratory chamber. Headlong, he dived for the transparent cubicle in the center and wrenched its hatch open.

LIKE a wave of slime, the ourobos belched forth, spilling across the floor in a hideous, writhing blot.

The foremost of Vydys' charging guards screamed and tried to stop.

Too late. He pitched into the fungous tide; screamed just once more.

A bubbling scream...

The room erupted into chaos. Alike, Vydys' men and Zenaor's fled in shrieking panic.

Craig thrust a foot across one's path; snatched a fire-gun as the man fell sprawling.

The room was empty, then...empty save for dead Vydys and her guard, and Zenaor, and Narla, and Craig Nesom.

And the ourobos.

Coolly, Zenaor stood his ground beside the cubicle. Ourobos swept in close about his feet, then eddied back. They would not touch him.

He laughed; gestured. "You see, alien? The tanagree oil is in my veins; they will not touch me. But you..." He laughed again.

Craig said, "Much good may it do you Zenaor. A corpse is a corpse, even if the worms won't eat it."

He raised the fire-gun.

Zenaor's laughter died. He half-turned. "Wait, Earthman—"

He whipped up his own weapon.

Craig fired.

Zenaor died.

Then Narla was in the Earthman's arms again, heedless of the ourobos' creeping tendrils. "So we die, Craig Nesom. But at least we die together."

Craig held her close. "No, Narla."

"No—?" He could feel her body stiffen. "But—what—?"

"I said no, Narla. We don't die. Neither of us."

She stared at him.

He said, "Don't you see? The ourobos—they're thallophytes. That's the answer." And then, when she still showed no comprehension: "Tumek knew. That's why he said his crystal was the only weapon that would stop them. And Bukal hit it right—by accident—when he looked at the thing and said it might as well be a lamp lens."

"Craig, I don't understand—"

"I'll show you." Pushing the girl back, Craig took the jewel case from the table where Vydys had tossed it and crossed to the nearest lamp...carefully replaced the focus prism with the crystal.

The beam sprayed out, all green and purple.

Tilting the lamp, Craig brought it to bear on the encroaching slime of the ourobos.

Before his and Narla's very eyes, the creatures shriveled. The gray wave drew back.

Craig clipped, "This crystal concentrates some ray that's deadly to the ourobos, just as on my world quartz glass lets ultraviolet pass. That was Tumek's great secret. Somehow, he discovered Zenaor's plans and then worked out this incredible, yet simple solution.

Now, Baemae craftsmen can duplicate the formula and produce crystals by the thousands. It means the end of the ourobos."

He moved the light.   More gray slime dried to sticky viscous blackness.

Then, arm in arm, together, he and Narla walked out into Yoh's bright noonday light, shining down on the free-world-to-be of Lysor.

THE END

If you've enjoyed this book, you will not want to miss these terrific titles...

ARMCHAIR SCI-FI, FANTASY, & HORROR DOUBLE NOVELS, $12.95 each

D-21   **EMPIRE OF EVIL** by Robert Arnette
THE SIGN OF THE TIGER by Alan E. Nourse & J. A. Meyer

D-22   **OPERATION SQUARE PEG** by Frank Belknap Long
ENCHANTRESS OF VENUS by Leigh Brackett

D-23   **THE LIFE WATCH** by Lester Del Rey
CREATURES OF THE ABYSS by Murray Leinster

D-24   **LEGION OF LAZARUS** by Edmond Hamilton
STAR HUNTER   by Andre Norton

D-25   **EMPIRE OF WOMEN** by John Fletcher
ONE OF OUR CITIES IS MISSING by Irving Cox

D-26   **THE WRONG SIDE OF PARADISE** by Raymond F. Jones
THE INVOLUNTARY IMMORTALS by Rog Phillips

D-27   **EARTH QUARTER** by Damon Knight
ENVOY TO NEW WORLDS by Keith Laumer

D-28   **SLAVES TO THE METAL HORDE** by Milton Lesser
HUNTERS OUT OF TIME by Joseph E. Kelleam

D-29   **RX JUPITER SAVE US** by Ward Moore
BEWARE THE USURPERS by Geoff St. Reynard

D-30   **SECRET OF THE SERPENT** by Don Wilcox
CRUSADE ACROSS THE VOID by Dwight V. Swain

ARMCHAIR SCIENCE FICTION CLASSICS, $12.95 each

C-7   **THE SHAVER MYSTERY, pt. 1**
by Richard S. Shaver

C-8   **THE SHAVER MYSTERY, pt. 2**
by Richard S. Shaver

C-9   **MURDER IN SPACE** by David V. Reed
by David V. Reed

ARMCHAIR MASTERS OF SCIENCE FICTION SERIES, $16.95 each

M-3   **MASTERS OF SCIENCE FICTION, Vol. Three**
Robert Sheckley, "The Perfect Woman" and other tales

M-4   **MASTERS OF SCIENCE FICTION, Vol. Four**
Mack Reynolds, "Stowaway" and other tales